The Sock in Karl Kerstensen's Shoe

Stories

Nina Zhelyazkova

Fomite
Burlington, VT

ISBN-13: 978-1-953236-62-3
Library of Congress Control Number: 2021953209

Fomite
58 Peru Street
Burlington, VT 05401
www.fomitepress.com
01-05-2022

Contents

I started looking for Karl's sock. And that's how I ended up here, in all those places…

The Red Sweater Found on Liberty Avenue

I had no intention of doing it at all. Damn, these things are totally not my style. But one day, walking down Liberty Avenue, I saw a red sweater.

It was scarlet red, just the way I like it. It was hanging from the back of a bench; sleeves touching the ground.

I wondered if anyone would come back for it. I wouldn't want to take anything special from anyone. Then I imagined it belonged to some stinky rich girl who would never go looking for her lost sweater.

With that thought, I took it from the bench. First I tied it around my waist, then I covered it as much as I could with my coat. I walked quickly. Some almost ridiculous fear took me over, that the owner of the sweater would in just a second walk down the street looking for it, would see its sleeves sticking out of my coat, and would call me a "little thief." I would return it to her guiltily, looking down the ground, and continue on my way as I listened to some sort of a nasal contemptuous giggling behind me.

But nothing like that ever happened. I went back to the hostel, took off my blue sweater and tried out the new one. It was soft and warm. It fit me well and this colour suited me. I kept it on.

That same evening, I met Sasha. A Russian with brusque and choppy features, like cut out of a thick cardboard. Nose straight and sharp, lips thin and serious, and when he smiled, two rows of slightly crooked teeth that seemed to give a warning; hair soft and blond, but cut too short, as if to erase the last gusts of tenderness on purpose.

He was sitting on the couch with his friends. He invited me over. He poured me a glass of Portuguese liqueur. We talked a little about insignificant things. Then we watched a movie. During the first scene he pulled me towards him. He held me. And after just a little while his hands were all over my body. Even through the blanket we were wrapped in, you could see what he was doing.

I liked it, but I was ashamed. I whispered to him:

-Sasha. I work here. I don't want my colleagues to know.

He continued.

-Why are you like that?

-I like it that way.

I made him stop.

-Come to my room.

-But your friends are there.

-They are already asleep. They won't notice.

-Sasha, I will not come.

The next day he texted me. They had moved into an apartment, which they had rented for a week.

-Do you want to come?

I wanted to go. I liked the way he touched me. There was not a drop of bashfulness in his hands. He was direct. Even rude.

The truth is that every woman wants the man with her to know what he is doing. This is the reason why seemingly harsh men succeed with women.

We want nothing more than to be protected. To know that, in his hands, we will find that support and security we have longed for our whole lives. But the brain confuses support and security with the sharp confidence of the sexual gesture. We find ourselves in the trap of a wish that will never come true.

How do I just go like that? I was aware that all Sasha wanted was to fuck me. No sentimentality, not even the false kindness of a dinner invitation.

Many men had offered me sex so far, but rarely so directly. It was insulting, this unadulterated crudeness of sincerity. He didn't even offer to pick me up. He just sent me a map with his location.

Maybe I was too naive to expect anything more. I knew that most men only wanted sex, but not all. There were those looking for something more. Holding hands, red sunsets and one or another shared passion for movies or books.

I, myself, wanted just sex. But not this way. Like any woman, I wanted to be courted first. A date invitation, a walk along the river, a glass of wine and maybe a few compliments. It is not so difficult to conquer a woman if she already likes you.

I liked Sasha and he knew it. But that wasn't enough.

-Do you want me to come right there? We can take a walk first.

-I prefer us to be alone at home.

At that moment, my desire to have Sasha evaporated completely. I told him:

-I'm sorry. I'm not coming.

-Why?

-Are you stupid? This is not the way to treat a woman. I expected a little more respect.

-What a shame.

-Excuse me?

-Sex would have been good.

I felt disappointed and a little hurt. I wanted to give him a chance, but that was the end. I had had only a little sleep last night, so I decided to go to bed. Sometimes all you need is a few hours of good sleep. It seems to serve as a barrier between two realities - the one before and the one after. If you want to change reality, all you have to do is cross it with a dream.

I woke up in the evening. I looked at my phone.

Nothing. Not even an attempt to apologize.

We live in the era of virtual communication. The previous generation used windows, and today's generation uses screens.

If your grandmother looks at the street and sees nothing there, not even a passer-by, then her life seems a little meaningless.

Similarly, if you sleep for a few hours and you still don't have a message at the beginning of the new reality, you start to feel anxiously lonely.

Sasha.

I was already cursing him in my mind. Idiot! Why does he think he's so special? So many men have tried to impress me, as sexy as him, and even more so. I wondered, I really wondered, if there was a girl in this world who would go through the humiliation to sleep with someone who was treating her this way.

I made myself a dinner, drank a glass of wine and completely forgot about this idiot. My shift at the reception was seven to twelve in the evening. It was a light shift. People either went to bed or chilled. Nobody wanted anything from me.

When work was over, I got ready for bed. I looked at my phone. Nothing again. A real idiot!

When you want to forget about something that happened, you can use a dream as a barrier between two realities. Every dream is an opportunity to start your life over.

But what if you can't fall asleep? Then you crash into the abyss of reality, which is hollow and black and has no way out. You feel the walls like a blind man, realizing they are not walls, but just air, new abysses of air you can cross without hindrance. But you are not looking for air, you're looking for cement, wood, plastic, whatever, some kind of a bottom to hold on to… Alas, there is nothing but new abysses of air, and the barrier you long for never appears. Alice in Wonderland, who never stops flying down, who falls and falls, the nightmare of reality, and sometimes all you want is to hit something hard. Falling, falling… For how long?

I had been struggling with the air for half an hour. And the Lisbon subway was closing at one in the morning. I still had time to catch it.

Where to?

When you want to forget about what happened, you can use a dream as a barrier between two realities. But what if you can't fall asleep?

Then you imagine you are sleeping. Everything that happens to you is just a dream.

Why do we all want to dream? Because deep down, everyone is a bit of a criminal. But at the same time, they are a bit of a coward.

The dreamer is without responsibility. That is why cowards prefer to dream. Only then can they afford to do whatever they want, without thinking about the consequences.

Even if you kill a person in your dream, you are innocent. Even if they kill you, you are alive.

And even if you become a call girl, you retain your dignity.

It was like a dream.

Where to?

I put on my new sweater. I put on lipstick the same color. I knew that Russian girls always dress up for a date, so I had to try harder if I wanted to impress him.

The only nice things I had were a black skirt and a pair of black tights. But the tights were torn on my toes.

I didn't have high-heels. I only had a pair of boots and a pair of blue sneakers. I put on my sneakers. Did I look good?

I didn't have too much time to think about it. I had to hurry.

I got off at Martin Munish station. I looked at the map on my screen. The first street perpendicular to this one. I went straight, just as Sasha had told me.

I felt sick on the first step. I wanted to go back. What was I doing on this street in the middle of the night, looking for the apartment of a total stranger?

I turned around. Then I remembered. That had been the last subway.

The first street perpendicular to this one and the first left.

And then? Number 56, he'd told me. It was dark and I couldn't see the numbers.

A woman walked down the street.

-Excuse me, miss, do you know where block 56 is?

She didn't know English. So I kept wandering, having no idea where to go.

I finally found it. Block 56. Now which apartment?

I looked at the chat. There was nothing about an apartment.

I looked at the names of the bells. There was one that didn't have a name. If they had rented an apartment for a week, the bell might not say anything.

I pressed it. Nothing. A minute. Two…

Someone showed up from the top floor. It was Sasha.

-Who is it? -he shouted.

I wanted to sink into ground. He wasn't expecting me.

-Nina.

He didn't answer. The window briskly shut. I was standing in front of the block door and I didn't know what to do. Five minutes later Sasha opened.

There was no elevator. We were both silent. Each new step was another drop of excitement hitting the ground.

When we reached the top floor, the Earth felt flat.

His friends were sitting on the couch. There were about six boys. We knew each other from the night before. Everyone knew what I had come for, and that made my humiliation even greater.

His room was across the living room. We went inside. He started undressing me.

First he took off my blue sweater. I had put it on top of the red one, because it was winter. Portuguese, but still winter.

Then the red sweater, the bra, the skirt. He started to take off my tights.

-Wait! -I told him.

-What's wrong?

-I'll do it.

When you have sex with someone you love, you don't care if he sees your imperfections. On the contrary, you want to show them to him, as to prove your love in a special way. You just tell him, "I trust you." This is the whole difference between love and porn.

But sometimes you hide the hole on the toes of your tights and this is when you realize that you don't care about him at all. You turn off the lights as soon as possible. Then you get under the sheets. You have passionate, beautiful, superficial sex.

But it's just a dream. You can do whatever you want. You can be up or down, change positions. But one thing you can't do. You can't change the way you feel. I didn't feel anything for Sasha and therefore I didn't feel anything during sex. I knew it would be like that from the very beginning. But I had decided to do it. It was as if I was not even there. I watched it all from outside, like a movie.

At least once in her life, every woman has fantasized about being raped. Again, the brain's confusion between support and security with the sharp confidence of the sexual gesture.

She's not ready, but he doesn't even ask her. He penetrates her slowly and hard. Moral rape. She doesn't want him, but she came to him herself. And as he penetrates her, she slowly begins to moisten. She likes that he wants her so badly that he is not even ready to comply with her. She likes the roughness of male passion. She is wanted.

No. Her body is wanted. No. Her vagina is wanted. Her thoughts: "Any other girl could be here, in my place." There is nothing special about Sasha's decision to bring her to bed. A matter of circumstances. A collection of coincidences. There is no difference between her and the other girls for him. There's something amusing about female vanity -- it makes a woman believe that she is special to her suitor.

Her thoughts - "There is something cruel in all men. How heartless is it to reduce the existence of a woman to only a single organ? How heartless is it not to care what lies in the averted gaze of her eyes? Maybe somewhere there, at the bottom of her eyelids, a story is beginning to form, a story he would never suspect of and never read."

Before, she wanted to sleep only with boys who found excitement in her thoughts. And suddenly she started to prefer only those who don't want to know anything about her thoughts. There is something way too comfortable about casual sex. She does someone a favor and he does a favor to her. Hearts remain whole and unaffected, and the needs of the body are met. Does having casual sex make her a whore?

Surely Sasha's friends, who are still sitting on the couch listening to her moans, would call her that. Surely, as soon as she pulled on her blue sweater and said "Goodbye" out of pure courtesy, he would call her that.

But what does a "whore" mean? A woman who sleeps with random men? A woman who uses men and then abandons them? A woman who sleeps with men for money? The mother of every man with an inferiority complex?

Where does femininity end and prostitution begin? Or for some men, like Sasha, are the boundaries completely blurred? It's something like conjunctivitis or a strange form of color blindness. Some men start sleeping with so many women that they stop seeing women as individuals. For them, all women are just bodies for fucking.

And if so, what was the reason she went to him? Does she not care what people think or is it that something deep inside of her has always longed to be humiliated?

If we want to forget about what happened, we use a

dream as a barrier between two realities. Maybe that's why when even two complete strangers find themselves done with the sexual intercourse, they prefer to call on the barrier, and only then to separate.

I wake up. A sunny room, a boy sleeping next to me. I put on my torn tights, my skirt, my sweater…

I am in a hurry to leave. I go through the living room. A few bottles of Portuguese liqueur, unfinished. The door is unlocked. "How convenient."

I'm a little bit late for my shift, but no one notices. After five minutes, the reception phone rings.

-Hello?

-Yes, please.

-Can we book a room for seven people?

-Of course.

I remember I have forgotten my blue sweater and a sock.

When Prague Became Homeless

I met Elishka on a cold winter afternoon. We were both working for some bar in Prague. I had started a little while ago and she - a little after. We had to hand out leaflets, damn it. Such a boring job, but you meet interesting people. As soon as I saw her, she caught my attention. You know, this is one of those moments when you feel that a person is special to you even before you know them.

We were out there in the cold square in this fucking winter, trying to jump away the cold. Me – a bit less, she- a bit more. Elishka was such a tiny creature, such a small thing - like an elf. Even her face was a bit like that - a bit elfish. With pronounced but gentle features, some freckles scattered like pollen, and some blond curls running down her forehead. I wanted to hug her and take care of her, I don't know why. She was a real elf, but she was lost.

We started having some of those long, insightful conversations that only happen when you meet somebody for the first time. Everything she told me was fascinating, but what grabbed me the most was:

-I worked at Subway, but I left on the first day. Do you know why? We worked at some large table and we had to cut the vegetables into a specific shape. If a piece was not cut perfectly, we had to throw it in the bin. And I thought, "What the hell, people have to be crazy to throw away so much food just because it doesn't look perfect. That is sick. I can't work here anymore."

Maybe for some people this short story would seem funny. At the end of the day, what's so fascinating about some girl leaving work on the first day because of some rules for cutting vegetables? If you don't understand what my enthusiasm is due to, I would not be surprised. But then I will ask you not to read further, because then obviously you will not understand anything about my little, little Elishka.

Elishka had lived in many places. At first she lived in Prague, she liked to call herself "a Prague girl" and she was proud of it. Then, when she grew up, she left for Australia, where her mother was from. "I miss the Australian sun. That's what I miss more than all. "-she liked to tell me. She went to college, but never finished it. She left, I don't remember why... Then she went again to I don't know where and finally returned, again, to Prague, where she did I don't know what...

I told her that we should exchange contacts and go out again sometime, because otherwise who knows when we'll see each other again. She gave me hers and I wrote her once, but she never answered.

One day my friend Sarah and I went to Mala Riba. It was her favorite bar and she was taking me there every week. It was kind of a tradition. We used to drink beer and talk about boys. Sara ordered a big beer, I - a little one and then another. And then another. I had just started telling her about this boy, XX, when we saw Elishka sitting alone at the bar. Sarah also knew her. They had been friends for many years and there was no way we could just pass her by. We sat with her. Then we talked for some long time. Elishka kept interrupting me, as if she had already grasped my thought and had no time to wait. But I wasn't angry with her for that. It was nice to have someone from time to time to understand you without explaining everything.

Then we went to a rock concert of Sarah's sister's boy-friend. On the way to the concert, we drank some wine that Elishka had carried in her bag. I asked her when she was plan-ning to go home and her eyes, all of a sudden, turned from elfish to ghostly.

This was one of those faces that are hard to describe in words. At one point, your delicate skin wrinkles between your eyebrows and your whole childish face shrinks as if something bad has just happened. It all lasts only a second.

-Got it. And for how long has it been like that?

-I don't know. It's not the first time I run away from home.

-But how will you stay outside in this winter?

-I have wine. And I know all the bars in town.

Oh, Elishka. I wanted to take her with me, but there was no way. I didn't live in my own place, but in the apartment of a colleague, Ethan, for about two weeks.

I told her I would still ask Ethan if she could stay with us. She shouted:

-No, no, no... I don't want everyone to know about this!

We were sitting in some smoky bar in the suburbs of Prague; we got there by tram without buying a ticket. Sarah was already gone, it was just me, Elishka and all the cigarette smoke in the world. I was sick. I was suffocating, but we couldn't go out because it was really cold and the only thing I could do was stay in that bar with her, keeping her company until the night faded away. Nasty, nasty, stupid situation.

I told her:

-Don't worry. Ethan is a good man and I don't believe he would refuse.

Elishka swayed between wanting to maintain her reputation and rest after all this long fucking night.

In the end, I still wrote to Ethan. He saw it and didn't answer. Elishka repeated:

-No, don't insist. I found a friend I could go to.

-Really?- I asked.

She assured me that was the case.

I didn't know whether to believe her or not. But in the end my own fatigue prevailed. My throat hurt terribly and I was needing fresh air, so I asked her again:

-Will your friend really take you home?

-Yes, really.

And so we said goodbye. I was feeling terrible about Elishka, mostly because I didn't know what I could do. I saw her at work again a day or two later. She told me that she had spent all her money and had not eaten for two days. I dragged her to the store and bought her some food. Damn, I should have bought her more.

Elishka was getting worse and worse. Every night she wondered where to stay. I kept her company in the bars; from time to time, I bought her something to drink because she had no money and, to be honest, she was addicted to alcohol. If I refused to buy her something, she would start asking people around her if they could get her a drink, and one of them would finally agree.

So one early morning in an almost empty club that was closing, where we were already fighting with the staff, to stay a little longer before getting kicked out, playing the patience game (and Elishka had been forced to learn how to play this game very well) she told me about her whole family and why she didn't want to go home.

Her mother and father were divorced, and her mother was married to another man. He was beating Elishka and her brother on daily basis, but mostly her because she was the most stubborn. I looked at that girl and thought that if there was one thing she could be proud of, it was that she was still stubborn, that even though someone had tried to break all that fire in her, her fire was still burning and burns on ceaselessly. Such a fire was way too rare. Only then I realized what was so special about Elishka.

Then she told me that her father also lived in Prague. He was very old, twenty years older than her mother and suffered from some disease, I no longer remember what. He sat at home like a vegetable, almost didn't speak; there, in that house it was very, terribly cold because her father had no money for heating. "I can't go back there, to that house. It's all so cold in there…"

So, this was briefly the reason for Elishka's homelessness. Those waves of despair, when her face changed its whole shape and depicted all the childhood helplessness of the world, still kindled the fractions of the seconds. Seconds of most unexpected places - trams, bars, discos, Mexican food kiosk chains and squares of unheard names. She remained still just as small, just as innocent as an elf, and yet just as lost as before.

There was a saying, "There can be no friendship between two women, one of whom is very well dressed." If I had to paraphrase it, I would say, "There can be no friendship between two girls, one of whom is homeless."

But I wanted the friendship between me and Elishka to continue. That's why I often became homeless myself. Sometimes I was getting sick of all those bottomless evenings, like falling into a hole from "Alice in Wonderland". I was getting sick of having to buy two beers, or feeling guilty if I ate food. But even in such cases, I knew that people who leave Subway just because they don't want to throw away vegetables should be kept like the retina of your eyes.

So, on New Year's Eve, Elishka got kicked out of our bar as well. This happened because she was starting to break down little by little, and no one understood why. No one but me. And all this fire, and all this hell she was burning in, they found funny, and she herself didn't understand why. Just as the children don't understand why they are being accused of their deeds.

Elishka was somewhat shameless. She didn't know what it meant to listen to others till they finish their sentence, let alone follow the rules. But that's exactly the right word — she didn't know. And if you try to show her, you better stay away from her. She won't let anyone teach her how to live. Even if she makes mistake after mistake, she still won't take your advice. Everyone would call this stupidity, stubbornness. But there is something else. There is some force in adults with the behavior of children, some force which they themselves do not suspect. But in society, upfront behavior is considered a disadvantage.

What was it that made Elishka behave so edgily? Her stupidity, her innocence, or her fear of people doing to her what her stepfather has been trying to do for so long? Her fire, maybe? But fire, just as much as it can kill, can give life. People don't realize that. People look at the fiery man and kick him out, just like that. Maybe they are afraid, but in this fear, they are doomed to death.

So, Elishka lost her job. But not long after, money came to her from somewhere and she rented a room in some apartment. She invited me to come over. I was so happy for her, that she was no longer on the street. She had just moved in and there were piles of plates in the sink, built up by her two roommates.

We were washing dishes for at least an hour. It may sound strange, but that made me happy. Then Elishka made some spaghetti and said:

-This is for the time you bought me bread.

We ate spaghetti and drank wine. She told me she had a hole in her stomach.

-What?

-I have a hole in my stomach. I don't know what it's called.

-An ulcer.

-Yes. Ulcer.

-Maybe you should stop drinking.

And she looks at me with her stubborn eyes. But I say it with my best intentions and she knows it.

-Yes, maybe.

I know that Elishka has an ulcer from alcohol and stress, but there's something else, too. She has a hole somewhere else and it is getting harder and harder to fill it…

Then we go to a bar, the one we met in for the first time. We share a glass of beer and I hurry to leave. Although I love Elishka, I can't stand all this fire, sometimes it tires me out terribly bad.

We say goodbye, and the next day I leave for Portugal. She tells me: "Please, come back again and visit me. You can sleep at my place."

I send her a postcard, which she is looking forward to. In the end, she doesn't seem to have received it.

Once we manage to hear each other on Skype and re-kindle our friendship with occasional texting.

She asks me: "Come on, when are you coming to Prague?"

Months pass. Five, six…

Finally, it's time to go back to Prague. I'm writing to Elishka, but she seems to have abandoned her profile. I ask Sarah if she knows anything about her. She tells me: "I can't contact her either. The last thing I heard was that she might have gone to South America…"

And so, damn it, Prague suddenly becomes homeless.

Two Cups Of Chocolate and a Few Pieces Of Cake

We met at Vzorkovna. This was a bar in the center of Prague, where they played live rock music every night and served the drinks in glass jars.

I noticed him the first time he passed around. I thought he was handsome and I went to talk to him. In general, I don't do such things. But I was already a little drunk and that's why I didn't care too much, even if I screwed it up.

I don't know why I always think I'll screw it up. What boy wouldn't want to be approached by a medium pretty, medium tall 19-year-old girl?

His name was Daniel. Ukrainian. He had a gentle face and a sarcastic smile. From those who always treat life with a hint of ridicule because they've been through too much. I don't know what color his eyes were. It was dark and everything around was losing color.

It was hard for me to believe that he was 33. If he hadn't told me, I would have thought he was my age.

I remembered the American businessman who had spoken to me an hour earlier. He was 30, and the shadows of death were already dancing on his face.

What a relative thing age is! Some people start aging before they have passed half of their lives, while others stay the same for life. I thought the only real age is the one of the heart.

Daniel looked just like a boy and behaved like one. He was a little naive, a little shy and very charming. He told me he was an artist and loved colors. I was treated to an apple cider and then we went dancing.

When the first song was over, he kissed me.

-So you like me?- I asked him.

-Since I saw you.

Vzorkovna was closing. We had to go somewhere else. He offered to go for a hot chocolate and I agreed.

Some will say that Prague is most beautiful in the summer. Then everything blooms and the streets are full of life. It's like walking through a scarlet poppy that keeps unfolding.

But nothing can compare to the night streets of Prague in winter. Then it's cold and foggy, so no one goes outside.

If by chance someone happens to walk through the center in the middle of the night, it's only because they have to.

No romance, no causeless walks. And at four o'clock in the morning it is completely empty.

However, the streets are still just as narrow and covered with cobblestones. On each side you're welcomed by lavish windows with treats and souvenirs. The street lamps still shine just us nicely, but not out of vanity.

And if a boy and a girl happen to disturb the frozen peace of the streets of Prague, the quiet tunnels sing, colored by loneliness, and all the lanterns shine only for them. Everything is made just for the two of them, so winter is the most romantic season.

Daniel stopped in front of a small pastry shop with wooden doors. They groaned softly as he pushed them. We went inside.

It was a real childhood dream. It was full of chocolates, candies and all kinds of delicious things.

He poured me a cup of hot chocolate.

-Won't they fire you?

-I don't care.

We were sitting in the empty pastry shop, just the two of us, and talked until it was time for the first subway. Then he saw me off. We didn't have time to kiss goodbye.

It was a good night. I would say magical. However, I did not intend to see him again. I believed that such lucky coincidences of fate could not be repeated.

The New Year had passed. I was still in Prague thinking about him. I couldn't get Daniel out of my head.

I found him on Facebook. Daniel Savchuk, Artist. From Lviv, Ukraine …

I don't know why, but some cool small tears started flowing from my eyes. I wrote to my friend Sarah, who already knew everything about the night. "Do you remember Daniel? … Yeah, the same one. By the way, he's married."

No, these were not tears of sadness. That's how you cry out of sarcasm.

Has it ever happened to you? The situation seems so ridiculous that you just have nothing to do but shed a few tears and then start laughing.

"Yes, Sarah, I didn't expect that either. Such are the shortcomings of 33-year-old men. At one point, it turns out they are all married and have a child."

"Hey, are you all right? You will be fine, forget it. " Sarah wrote.

She obviously didn't understand my sense of humor. Everything was fine with me. Tears were dripping out of my eyes and I was laughing out loud. I just wanted to get her to laugh for a while with me.

Both Elishka and Sarah agreed that I should forget him.

I believed the same. However…

First, I wanted to ask him why he didn't tell me about that.

Not out of curiosity or an attempt to justify him.

I wanted to ask him to defend my honor.

Or, in fact, I didn't want to ask him any questions. I wanted to tell him straight away, "Daniel, I know you're married. You thought you were going to hide it from me, but I'm not that stupid."

I wanted to show him that I wasn't stupid and leave it there.

However, in order to do such thing, you have to be a real idiot.

First, I lacked the courage to meet him again. I had to go into the pastry shop and ask his colleagues about him. That way everyone would know there was something between me and him. They would whisper to each other "who is this girl, looking for Daniel?" They would think I am crazy, desperate, or worse - in love.

But that wasn't all. What if it wasn't his shift? Then I would leave the shop with a long face and I would never come back because I would die out of shame if I had to look for him again in the same place.

Or worse! He could be there. What would I do then?

I stood in front of the cafe for ten minutes, thinking through all the possible scenarios. Then I left. I swore I would never set foot on this street again. Maybe they had already seen me. I must have looked like a mad girl preparing to do something strange. If I came back, I would make myself look completely ridiculous. Daniel must have seen me already and was giggling in some corner. Everyone probably already knew I had something to say to him.

Then I went to my friend, Cecilia. She was a bartender and always poured me some free alcohol. The cheapest, but still, it was something.

I drank the two glasses of mediocre white wine. Then I went back to the cafe. Two decisive breaths and went inside.

-Is Daniel here?

-Yes, in the other room.

-Thanks.

-Daniel!

-Nina! Come here, sit down. Do you want something to drink?

-Well… bring me some hot chocolate.

He brought it to me.

-Look, I wanted to talk to you. Do you have time?

-Not much, but tell me.

-Sit down, please.

He sat down.

-Tell me… why didn't you mention that you are married?

-Not really. I did it just for the documents.

-But you have a child.

-I have four.

I was surprised, I admit it. I didn't expect such plot development.

-How is that possible? You've only been together for a year…

-They are all from different women.

-But you are still very young. How old were you when you had your first child?

-I was young.

-How young?

-I was very young.

Daniel started laughing. I laughed too.

-I was 17… And now he, Giovanni, is that old.

-You know, then your son and I are almost the same age.

-I know. I know… -Daniel repeated and laughed again.

-But Daniel… You can't just have children like that. You have to take care of them, for fuck's sake! Children mean responsibilities.

Daniel didn't answer.

-Do you understand, children must have a father?

He looked at me with eyes full of tenderness and warmth.

But there was something else. It was tenderness and warmth, mixed with a strange dose of sarcasm. A kind of curious and at the same time very painful sarcasm.

Blue. His eyes were blue.

-Do you take care of them at all? How often do you see them?

Daniel didn't answer again. He just looked at me with his smile, as if I were one of his children, asking too many questions. Then he took a napkin from the table and wiped the hot chocolate off my lips.

-Daniel, are you listening to me?

-Что же ты меня лечишь, деточка?

-I don't understand what that means.

Daniel could no longer speak. There was a woman who wanted to pay her bill and then he had to arrange the pieces of cake on the counter.

And who would arrange my own pieces?

A Tree Like Any Other

A tree like any other. Nothing special. You climb to the top of the hill. There is a path that leads to the Valley of Sharon, if you are curious enough to follow it. From there you can see "Alhambra" and a glimpse of my valley, where I lived with a group of nomads. You will hardly be impressed, even if you go down there. You will see only a cave with simple pieces of clothing placed around the entrance to protect you from the mountain cold at night, an umbrella, one of those beach umbrellas, but torn apart, a few mattresses scattered around, if they are still there at all, and a hammock stretched between two trees. That was Three's hammock (not that it matters to you).

-And the tree?

Oh, yes. That tree, right there, at the top of the hill. It's neither very big nor very small. I don't remember what kind of tree it was, maybe olive. I'd have to check if one day I gather the strength to go back.

Then I will probably be either very old, so old that I would have forgotten, or James will be with me. This, the latter, is highly unlikely.

In fact, my story is way too stupid. One night James and I climbed the top of the hill. Everyone in the cave was asleep, but still, just in case. We put the blanket under the tree, I lifted my skirt and he lay on me. We did it out of curiosity. It was just some stupid experiment. How would it feel like making love on a top of a hill under a tree that has no name? We were both cold. After all, the morning was slowly approaching, and the mornings in the mountains are colder even than the wee hours of the night.

We went back to the cave and fell asleep shortly before the moon began to fade. It was our first night together; we would say "a matter of consequences". It happened so that James lay down next to me and we both couldn't sleep, so we talked for a while, for more than a few hours; then at one point we stopped talking. I hadn't known him for a long time. I only knew he was playing guitar on the street. That's how I saw him for the first time. His eyes didn't really say anything, they were just speechless of some sorrow. Then I wanted to hug him, but it was too early. He wanted the same but smiled to me instead.

Since then, I started looking for him every day. All those guitars that crossed my path were dumb. Only his was not, but it didn't call me from anywhere.

One day I met him again. He introduced me to the other nomads and I moved in with them. This was the beginning of some crazy days… We all slept until late. Most days we didn't even know until when, because none of us had a watch. Our phones had been dropped on the ground, somewhere between the pockets of our dirty tracksuits, and the soil dug up by the forest dogs.

Little by little we woke up. First it was Clouds and Pete, who were already lighting the fire to make the first cup of coffee. Then it was James and me, we had already woken up, but we were kissing and falling asleep again, like newborns looking for each other's lips instead of food. When we heard 'coffee' we rushed to the fire, for it was not known if any would remain if we waited a little longer. Cuba and Mikey were already around the fire, and Three and Shaquille were sticking their heads out of the hammocks stacked on top of each other between the trees next to the fireplace. Look at those scoundrels! They were best off. All they had to do was reach out their hands to get their breakfast.

Our rush, as always, had been in vain. Here, even the simplest things are initially a set of complex plans. Leon is still collecting kindling for the fire, the water is not even put to boil. But we've made the mistake of getting up, so we stay with the others. James starts playing his guitar, then Mickey and Clouds, but not together, each with their own little tune. James stops only when the cigarette reaches him - it is then I try to steal some of his attention. I do this in a foolish way, almost like the small children. I tie something in his dreads, a twig or a piece of cloth hanging from my hand or I just pull his hair. He almost looks at me and asks me 'you all right?', this stupid question that the English always ask, of course I'm all right, James, but I want a bit more than this cold question, for fuck's sake! I know he's not in love with me and that, little by little, I'm starting to fall for him or fuck it, I've already sunk, no matter how much I don't want to admit it. I can't expect anything from him and he says it. He himself can't expect anything from me. We are both just nomads, vagabonds with no purpose or destination. All of life is here and now, and even if it sounds good to unite our paths, we both knew from the very beginning that we will not do it. This is a question we've not even discussed. He can read it in my eyes. They are dark even by daylight, and if by chance a green spark flashes in them, it is still dark, dark as my independence and only the wind can light it up. I could never travel with him, not even if he happens to be the fucking love of my life. He does not want me enough. His blue eyes do not say anything, and only infuriate the hell out of me. When I look at them, I see nothing, not even speechlessness of some sorrow. Then I pull his hair even harder and he does not understand, he does not understand that while he is playing his guitar and almost looking at me, little by little, I start sailing north.

Please, James, just get mad. Then I'll promise you I'll never think of Barcelona again. I'll drop all my plans, I'll stay with you, I'll keep disturbing you and admit that I love you. I want to see only one storm, but one that throws even the poor dolphins ashore. Don't worry, they'll only be there for a while. Then I'll pass and calm them down, I'll bring them back to the sea where they belong.

But James continues to play his guitar.

A long time has passed. (We don't know exactly how much.) We make breakfast. Sometimes we have a whole bag of pastries, I'm not kidding, plenty of cakes, croissants and donuts. We are all pros at dumpster-diving. We know where the best bakeries in town are and where they throw away their unsold treats, and the more hands, the more the breakfast. But we are not so great at planning. Some mornings we have nothing but fucking hard bread, and one morning we didn't have that either. Nothing, just onions, plenty of good fresh onions…What can be done with so many onions? James started cooking. First, he made the base of a French onion soup, which remained unsouped, and then he added all the crumbs and seeds we collected from the sacks full of bread a few days ago. Then I found two decent carrots and some beetroot in the trash and voilà - an onion salad. You could call us anything you wish…but you can't deny we could turn nothing into something.

Finally, with full or irritated stomachs, we were going down to the city, each on their own business. Some went to play music on the streets, some to juggle, and I danced from time to time. We had plans to do a big show on the street, all together and each doing whatever they can. Once they almost came true, but it was then when my heart started aching more and more often.

I danced less and less each day. The storm I was always anticipating never came. I was already starting to wonder if there were any dolphins in the sea at all. One morning I packed all my stuff, put on my backpack and said I was going somewhere, I don't know where. It was time for me to start healing.

I returned two days later, still sick, my eyes swollen with fatigue and dead-end flights. I sat by the fire. The others were sucking pieces of bread.

"I'm leaving for Morocco in five days," James told me.

I threw my backpack into the cave, went back to him and looked at him without saying anything. Then I wanted to hug him, but it was too late. He wanted the same, but instead he looked at me, for the first time with some kind of feeling, I don't know what.

I had no idea where I would be in a week, but I knew I would be here for the next five days. It was one of those times when nothing made sense, love the least.

We never went to the tree at the top of the hill again. After five days he really left, and I stayed in the cave for some more long time. I didn't have the strength to move. The wind that blew north was still calling me, but I couldn't make any answer. And from the south there was not even a breeze, the Sahara desert was heartless. Out of all those nomads, I remained the most faithful to this valley. From a guest I became a hostess. Little by little, everybody was starting to leave.

I thought if there were fairies in the forest, then I am one of them. Maybe I'm going crazy. I'm alone here, surrounded only by ghosts of some love that will never return. And yet I look forward to the time when I could dance again.

One day I decided I couldn't wait any longer. I climbed the hill with my backpack, this time full of everything I needed, and said goodbye to the valley which was still waiting for someone to return, the poor old woman, deaf to even my own Goodbye, the last goodbye that echoed in her.

I arrived in Barcelona all alone. I met a girl who was a nomad just like me, but inexperienced, and I was proud to have known this craft for a long time. I showed her how to do dumpster-diving. You didn't have to dig through all the garbage, it was enough to throw a glimpse on the top. Very often there were ice cream cones, an unfinished box of potatoes or even a flattened croissant, still in package.

To find food in the trash is a whole art. Anyone can reach into a treasure chest and take out a jewel, but how many people can reach into the trash can and take out a jewel? You have to do it quickly, without many people noticing you, because that way you'll attract unnecessary attention. But in spite of everything you shouldn't give too much of a fuck. In order to do this job you have to be really nonchalant.

Then someone crossed my path. He didn't hug me passionately like in the movies. But when he smiled broadly at me, I knew at that moment he was here only for me, and I didn't need anything more.

You all right? You all right? I have a whole bag of croissants, let's have lunch!

We sat on the street like in the good old days.

-Where do you plan to sleep?

-On the street round the corner. Stay with me.

-No need, we can go to a hotel.

-Ha-ha, James, why's that?

-Look, these days Barcelona is madness. I made a bunch of money, you won't believe it…

It was so funny for both of us. The last months we had only slept on the ground, eaten food from bakery dumpsters and bathed in the river. Suddenly here we were, in this whole big room just for us, with clean white sheets on the bed and a huge bathroom where a long-forgotten shower awaited us. A lot of mud had to fall from my feet if they were to be called clean, but even then they remained brownish, the earth fresh and stuck inside the skin. Once the seal of nomadism has marked you, it remains incurable, and the valley I'd left forever would never leave me.

-Let's pretend we are rich! -I said, and wrapped all the white sheets around my body like a dress. I walked gracefully around the room. James was sitting on the bed, laughing. I started dancing.

We were making love. It was so different from the one under the tree at the top of the hill.

In Barcelona, the moon didn't shine so brightly, it was almost invisible. Early in the morning we did not have to snuggle closer to each other, hands clasped in each other's bodies so as not to get cold. We did not even wake up from the cold, we just woke up out of laziness, not knowing whether it was day or night, each in their own blanket, in their own part of the bed.

One day my heart started aching again, I don't know why. I was lying on the bed. I had just taken a bath and I was waiting for my body to dry. The drops were running down my skin, which smelled of sandalwood and orange, my hair had recently started to shine, shaking off all the dust and scent of ashes, and the dirt in my heels, though still there, was beginning to fade. I was clean, clean as a baby's ass, but my soul heavy with slag.

I started to cry. I couldn't control myself — I was torn by convulsions. James ran to me, tried to calm me down and asked me what was going on. I kept shivering from cold, but it wasn't the cold that used to wake me up in the valley. It was coldness I couldn't explain. Then I told James I want him, he told me he was here with me, I told him I wanted him inside me and he promised me that we will make love, but he still didn't get it, I told him that I want him in me always, forever. I cannot stand that we live in two different bodies. I cannot stand we live in two different bodies. I'm in pain. My whole body hurts. Everything hurts, do you understand? The space between me and you hurts. Even when we make love, there's still space between us, I can never heal that space. He told me that everything would be fine. I kept crying. I was no longer in pain, I was just cold.

The next day I left for Morocco. James was still asleep on his side of his bed. I didn't want to wake him up. I just wanted to run away.

I had to rush, to escape, I don't know where, but I just had to run away from here, from the man that hurts so much.

Once again my hair is covered with ashes and dust. The smoke of a thousand fires has dug its nails into my hair and left its mark forever. My feet got coated by sand. Not the sand of the valley, but another type of sand, sand much drier, sand in which no tree could ever set roots. My eyes were still dark and no wind was there to brighten them up. I lived with other nomads, other men kept me warm in the crack of dawn. One morning - it was colder than ever - I unhooked my hands from the man who was holding me, and I went out of the tent. For the first time in a long time the wind was blowing. The Sahara began sticking to my face like a kiss-of-death shaman. All the dunes were empty, infinitely deserted. Not even the silhouettes of camels that walked slowly and carried the stormless skies on their humps were there. They were gone or maybe they were just sleeping somewhere, hidden behind the dunes. My body began to tear from convulsions, something broke in me and soon tore off forever; then I realized that James had been, although for just for a while, always in me.

Sugar

I saw Jordan for the first time rushing to the cathedral. Out of breath, red-nosed, and in a terrible hurry. The thing is, I had to meet Malika, that French witch who was teaching me to belly dance, and Clouds, the old American hippie who was going to play the clarinet for us. We were thinking of doing a small performance on the street. It had worked out once. Then Clouds was very late, but the fucker still came, and we made a whole ten euros for one hour, which we divided into four, because Kaze, that Spaniard with a Japanese name, had joined us, too.

I was whizzing through the narrow streets of Albaicín with the typical strides of an always-ready-for-news-adventures girl. It was five after five, and the cathedral was far away. Malika must have gotten there already, and alas, I had no phone to warn her that I was going to be late.

Jordan was sitting on the ground and singing with his

thick husky voice. It reminded me of honey, perfectly fragrant and ripe, but at the same time slightly bitter in a nice way.

I wouldn't have stopped if I hadn't seen Clouds. He was sitting next to him, playing his clarinet in poignant oblivion.

-Clouds! -I shouted at him.

-Oh, hello.-He looked up at me and finally noticed me.-This is my friend Jordan.

Jordan stood up and shook my hand warmly.

-¿Qué tal? -he asked briskly with his perky male voice.

Both his dark skin and his voice made everyone think he was Spanish. In fact, he was from Scotland. But he spoke the few Spanish sentences he knew with such confidence that even with the bunch of mistakes he was making, the Spanish complimented him on the language.

-Very well,- I said hastily, turning to Clouds again. -Clouds, did you forget we had a meeting with Malika at five?

-Oh, is it already five? -he asked in surprise.

-Yes, a quarter after five.

-Well, fine then.

And he slowly packed his luggage. Of course, so as not to offend Jordan, we invited him with us.

It was the week of Semana Santa, the craziest week of the year. Every afternoon there were huge processions all over the city, so huge that all the traffic was clogged. There were no cars, no streets without dead ends, in other words, no way to escape the damned procession without becoming part of it for an exhaustingly long period of time. People wore strange hats, reminiscent in all respects of those of the Ku Klux Klan. The truth is that the Ku Klux Klan had taken the idea from Catholic Passion Week, but Clouds, who liked to joke, added:

-Do you understand, guys, that you look like the most influential racist organization of the previous century? -and he laughed only the way Clouds could laugh. First, he exposed his teeth in a wide, goofish smile. Second, he directed his short, booming guffaw like a fifth-grader teasing his friend straight at you, as if waiting for confirmation of his silliness. Then everyone Clouds looked at laughed.

Clouds, Jordan and I were walking through the procession in complete despair. Clouds offered to take another street. After all, he claimed, he knew the city like the back of his hand, but even there the situation was tragic. We had no choice but to drag ourselves to the cathedral as if carrying an invisible cross. On the way, to have fun, we occasionally reached a hand into a trash can and took out some unfinished bottle of sangria, from which we drank.

"The good thing about holidays is, you can always recycle alcohol." -Clouds encouraged me and attacked me again with his laughter.

Finally, after an hour, we found ourselves in front of the cathedral. We circled it all around, and it was huge, so it took another hour. As you can guess, there was no sign of Malika.

All three of us were confused. We had come all this way crushed by inexplicable torments and in the end, we found ourselves without a plan again. Something had to be done.

-Let's go have a drink! -Jordan suggested.

-Well, okay.

I didn't know either Jordan, or Clouds too well. I had met Clouds one night while we were sitting in a circle on the ground in some park singing songs; he was the lead guitarist.

-I don't take any more orders for "Smells like teen spirit" or "Comfortably numb".- he joked.

Then we had to meet again when he came to our first show with Malika, because he had forgotten me.

-I meet too many people.

But of course, you can't ever get mad at a hippie.

So, this time, third time round, Clouds seemed to remember my name. He and I had no money, we had traveled for god knows how long, and Jordan, who had just come from Scotland, was spending paper recklessly here and there. He treated us to a beer and then went back to singing and playing his guitar on the street. We sat next to him.

-If you want, you can sing with me. - Jordan shouted at me. -We'll split the money. Or not, I'll give it all to you, no problem.

-I can't sing.

-It doesn't matter. If you want, you can sing.

But nothing worked right at this Semana Santa. You have to be a real madman to sing during a procession. I knew almost nothing about Jordan besides that he was very perky, kind of a show-off, probably macho, a spoiled Western European guy who comes to spend all his money on vacation and knows nothing about life. And, of course, always bursting with plans.

-Let's go to a hostel. I have two girlfriends from Israel there, I have to see them. They are very dear friends of mine. I met them yesterday and promised to see them again.

Clouds and I, like two free electrons, followed Jordan's mesmerizing voice. At the front desk, a woman stopped him and said:

-I'm sorry, I can't let you in this time. If you wish to sleep here, you'll have to pay.

Jordan began carefully flirting with her. It was obvious that the woman at this front desk was furious about something, and he, like some skilled lightning rod, was sending all the lightning back to the sky.

-But please, ma'am, I just want to see my dear friends from Israel.

-No. I can't let you sneak into the hostel anymore. If you want to sleep here, you'll have to pay.

-Look, madam, I have no such intention. I just need to

talk to them for five minutes. Is this a hostel or a prison? Five minutes…

-Five minutes.- she said warningly.

-Thank you, madam. What a kind young lady!

And we followed him, explaining that we go together.

The two dear friends from Israel soon came down and offered us coffee. We agreed and stayed there for a while. Half an hour later the girl from reception appeared, already determined to evict Jordan.

-This time we won't play it nice… There's no way I won't notice you if you stay on that couch.

-Oh, miss, excuse me for that night. Of course, we're leaving now.

All five of us left the hostel. The girls from Israel wanted us to go to some flamenco show in some cave.

-Where is this cave?

-We don't know. But sooner or later we'll find out.

We were wondering whether to accept this invitation or refuse it. Soon the problem resolved itself. We lost them in the crowd.

We set sail again, just the three of us - me, Jordan and Clouds. Now we had a new problem. We had to come up with a plan for the evening again.

-I suggest we recycle some food. - I said.

-What do you mean? - Jordan asked.

Clouds and I eagerly started explaining to him. "Ah- I thought condescendingly- this ignorant fella, who has no idea about these things."

On the ground I found a green apple covered with red sugar syrup. It was real happiness! Blessed be the clumsy child who dropped it without even biting it off, and his wasteful parents who took him to buy him a new one. I ran to the nearest fountain, overflowing with childlike enthusiasm, washed it, and went back. We shared it with Clouds, and Jordan didn't want any. I was asking myself why on earth he is still hanging with us, the two scoundrels, instead of getting drunk with some other tourists downtown.

At one point, the Israeli girls reappeared. They hugged and kissed Jordan as if they hadn't seen each other in a hundred years.

-Ah, we lost you! Where did you disappear?

-Well, we lost you too. So, are we going to go to that cave?

The old dilemma again. The three of us frowned and began to think. In general, Jordan and Clouds agreed on everything, so it was up to me to decide.

-I don't feel like going too much. Yes, on the one hand it sounds like fun, but on the other hand you don't know exactly where it is.

-We'll find out, sooner or later.

-I don't know, I'd personally recycle food.

In the end we just sat on the corner and ate stuffed potatoes, which the two girls bought for us. We ate well, but I had to recycle anyway. I had an appointment with Shaquille to check the bakeries around.

-Come with us.-I invited them.

Clouds came with me, and Jordan stayed with the two Israelis.

I saw him again a few days later, on the street again, singing Bob Dylan songs, better than Dylan himself, and that voice of his made all the girls turn. He greeted me warmly with a kiss on both cheeks, asked me how everything was, and invited me to sit next to him. "Don't think twice, it's all right..."

Then he suddenly asked me where I slept. I told him that I lived in a cave with a few boys, and he nicely asked me if he could stay there for the night if there was room.

I still didn't know what to think about Jordan. I was wondering why he would sleep in a cave and what kind of person he was. I was a little suspicious of him, but I'm like that with all machos with flirty manners. Still, I told him he was welcome. I had already shown the place to Clouds and he had recently moved in with us. It was a more than crazy bunch of scoundrels!

One night Jordan slipped into the cave when everyone was asleep and fell on the ground. I saw him and told him:

-Don't you at least want to cover yourself with something?

He had no sleeping bag or blanket.

-I don't want to bother you. It's spring, it's not so cold.

-But Jordan, please.

I couldn't watch him lie completely alone and helpless on the cold ground. I made room for him on my mattress and gave him something to cover himself. He fell asleep instantly.

This was the first and last night Jordan slept in our cave. I told him that he was always welcome, but alas, he did not have the strength to climb the hill every night. Most evenings he just slept in some bush, on a bench or just on the ground. All the money he made on the street he spent on alcohol and other stupid things.

We were walking down some street where a black woman was sitting on the ground selling hats.

-Do you want a hat?-he asked me.

-No. I don't need a hat.

-Come on, pick a hat.

-No, please.

-Then I'll pick it. Give me this one.

-Five euros.

-Take ten.

-Oh, Jordan, what do you need that stupid hat for?

-To help the poor woman. See how nice she is, and she has a daughter.

Another time he was playing with some guy named Tony.

I offered Jordan a peach, and he said:

-Oh, no, thanks. Tony, do you want a peach? Give it to Tony.

Or when he played with some girl, he was giving her all the money they earned.

Such a fool was Jordan, such a golden heart. He was too polite for someone to assume he was homeless, too generous to notice that he lived day to day, and too cheerful for you to think he might be an alcoholic.

Not long after, from being the chaotic boy I didn't trust, Jordan became my best friend. I often saw him playing on the street and sat next to him to listen to Bob Dylan, Jeff Buckley or Nina Simone, and what songs could have better suited Jordan than those of Nina Simone?

Sometimes it was just me and Jordan, sometimes it was me, Jordan and Clouds, me, Jordan and some girl who happened to be friends with him because he was friends with everyone, me, Jordan and Tony, this undisturbingly silent black Englishman who played the trumpet like the saddest cover of a jazz magazine, me, Jordan, and Rodrigo, the Mexican who was about to marry a Spanish gypsy just to learn to play the flamenco right.

There was no better feeling in the world than knowing that one sunny morning, as you go downtown on your business, you will find a friend to play for you. I felt especially proud to have a friend like Jordan. People were passing by, grabbing a few bars of his music. But no one else had the privilege of sitting next to the most talented and unknown musician in the world. He always smiled at them and blessed them. He really used the word "Bless!" every time someone passed by or said goodbye. And very often he exclaimed "Sugar!" He used to tell me: "My mother taught me that every time I wanna say a bad word, I should replace it with 'sugar.' I still do that today. You know, my mother died very young…"

I was thinking then what a treasure it is to have Jordan, to know the true meaning of simple words such as "sugar."

Not long after, I moved to another cave. It was closer to the city and there was no such hill-climbing as to the previous one. I knew I couldn't make Jordan stop drinking, but at least I could give him a chance to get somewhere home easier. That's why I told him:

-Move to my place.

He promised to do it. But my time in Granada was running out. I thought, "If I want to do one last thing in this city, it's to show Jordan where the damn cave is."

He often called me and asked:

-Hey, is it convenient for you to take me to this cave tonight?

-Yes, of course.

In the end, something always came up. And then

something else. And then something more. Jordan was always in the middle of some of his own vicissitudes, he could never organize himself to do a thing. He was the type of person who goes somewhere and meets someone on the way who makes them completely forget about their previous plans. When someone is addicted to something, he doesn't just give it up. And Jordan wasn't just addicted to alcohol. Jordan was addicted to sleeping on the cold ground, to his own painful homelessness. And while saying "sugar", while his mother was gone, he would still keep on being just as homeless.

I didn't want to tell Jordan that I was leaving soon. I didn't like saying goodbye. One night I saw him, he was going to a party. He looked very different -- he had cut his hair short. I asked him if he wanted a croissant and he, as always, refused. He blessed me and continued on his way. This is how I had wanted to see him for the last time. And Clouds, this head-in-the-clouds traveler, whom I never said goodbye to on my last night in Granada… He had said goodbye to too many people to feel sentimental about that one little girl who he had once shared a sugar-coated apple with. And such a farewell, without sentimentality, would have broken my little heart. Because he didn't know that I would always remember that ludicrous "Semana Santa" and his gray hair, disheveled like that of a hopeless youngster. But most of all, I would remember the blessed encounters with Jordan's voice before I'd turned the corner. And… sugar!

That's What You Deserve, Fucking Hippies

I, like most loners, have the terrible habit of falling asleep on the couch. One such afternoon, under my thin childhood blanket and with my small legs freezing, I fell into a fragile sleep. The year was 2020, the date was April 1st, and I was somewhere in the mountains, surrounded by fresh snow.

But who knows why my dream took me to another direction. I was in a cave, that same April, but in Spain, three years earlier. Stupid me, why did I ever leave?

I was right there, in this ridiculous cave, which was more like a hole in the rock, lined up with some pieces of clothing, we were sitting around some makeshift dinner served in large pots from hand to hand and listening to the stories of some lunatic who looked like a madhouse fugitive Jesus Christ.

But these stories were not wise parables, although some people equally affected by drugs thought they were, and sounded more or less as follows: "Me and the Virgin Mary, in the woods. I'll fuck you! There was nothing left. Then I took her pink purse.. Pink purse! Ahahahahaha! I will brush my teeth with butter…"

This shaggy, primitive man was an Italian, judging by his momentary outbursts in a foreign language, and we had picked him up from the street by mistake. If we have to be specific, *I* made this mistake because I really thought that he needed help, and not that we would all need help because of him.

So everyone was quiet, listening to the Italian's disconnected stories. There seemed to be a campfire, the wind outside made us snuggle a little closer together, and from time to time someone burst into sporadic laughter, which, like the sparks in the air, quickly faded with nervous anticipation of hearing more. And there was always more.

I was one of those who kept giggling. My laughter burned out sharply only when the food reached me. Then I grabbed two spoons and passed it on, greedily waiting for my turn again - if one came.

Dinner was over. Now, if we were in England. we would have a cup of tea. But since we were not all English, we decided to avoid national discrimination and perform the only ritual valid all over the globe -smoking weed.

The joint was passed just as slowly as the pot of mashed potatoes, but that didn't bother us. I was leaning against the rock - I remember that very well, because no one forgets its rough hug once he has tasted such bliss and misfortune. Finn was on my left , and on my right - I don't remember.

Finn was a boy I had met that night. I didn't live in this cave then - that would happen a little later. In fact, I had dragged myself there down the steep hill because of another boy, James. A little later, because of James, or rather because of the decision I made to be with him, my whole life changed.

But he didn't know this. He didn't realize that I had tortured myself descending a vertical surface just to drink tea with him. For some reason, a little later, the earth exerted its gravity through me to someone else. But don't think I fell in love with that someone.

No, I just liked the fact that he was the only one of this mixed group of losers to have read Hermann Hesse - if you don't count me, of course.

This someone shared with me a third of his blue sleeping bag, bought from Amazon for 10 euros - something that he himself boasted about. I think this is how our conversation began.

The other third of the sack was for Jerry, his curly-haired friend, who looked like a character taken out of Michelangelo's frescoes, one of his blond angels with a face that expressed something between self-repentance and boundless tenderness.

Jerry was there, but he didn't seem to be there — his function was not to be present in the conversation, but to watch it with compassionate empathy, without regard to its virtues or sins.

Finn and I had become steppe wolves long before we found ourselves in this cave. That's why there was no way we could be together - neither of us wanted to be Hermine.

Separately, we ran into the woods in pure delirium, hunting our prey with bare teeth, rubbing our feet into the sharp daggers of the river, and howling at the greyhounds as only really savage loners could howl.

My Hermine became James. Or rather, he became my Maria, because our relationship turned out to be perfectly short and fruitless, except that he poured a little life into my flimsy blood.

As for Finn - he taught me to steal. A quality no less valuable than being able to kiss.

For me, stealing had been a real taboo. Until one day I saw Finn and Jerry grinning in front of some supermarket.

"What did you do?" I asked them.

Jerry pulled a large triangular cheese with holes out of his inner pocket.

Of course, they didn't steal indiscriminately from here and there. They had a moral code.

• Do not steal your neighbor's cheese.

• Do not wish a cheese different than the one you own at the moment.

• Do not steal the cheese of the poor peasant, but only of the rich cattleman.

• Have no other cheeses besides the one you wish for truly with all your heart

• Do not kill for cheese…

And so on and so on…

But our friendship was not based solely on theft. It consisted of even greater adventures. We hung out on the street like professional losers. Finn played on a kind of a guitar, a kind of blues. Jerry and I chased away passersby with our drunken pirouettes. Then we lay down on the warm tiles and drank a kind of wine. This went on from morning 'till night. We were constantly giggling and laughing. In the evening we went on a hunt for sweets in the bakery dumpsters. There were hundreds of them in Granada. Our teeth dripped with chocolate. We'd never felt so loose, so carefree, so, literally, sweet. Finn kept on saying: "This city is like a projection of gypsy dreams, all together. And everyone comes here in mysterious ways to share their sublimated reality. "

From time to time some snobs came by to point their varnished fingers at us. But most people adored us because we were the most epic trio of all times. There was no and can be no dispute about it.

One day Maria left. Finn told me he'd been in love with me all that time. Sometime around then, the Italian set the camp on fire in a fit of rage.

"That's what you deserve, fucking hippies!" -some snob shouted at us from the top of the hill.

The three of us laughed a lot. At the end of the day, we had nothing important there. We mugged that guy, the daredevil up on top, and left him with his underpants only. They had gotten a little dirty.

All our cheese had burned, as had our frayed backpacks, five socks, parts of the sleeping bag, and about a hundred philosophers on top.

The Italian remained like the great Nero, watching his empire of rubbish slowly disperse. Standing, arms on his waist, naked against the wind waving his mighty flag before the world, he peed and left. We never saw him again, but the little squirrels told us he had moved with them into a hollow. They were feeding him acorns and he felt great. He had already begun to say related things. He'd regained consciousness. He had mentioned that his mother was from the foothills of Nazareth. Strange, this did not seem to be in Italy. Anyway. We let him go in peace or rather, vegetate in peace.

The three of us continued north — there was no further south to go. Finn and I never slept naked in his kind of sleeping bag. We promised to do it next summer. We vowed then to hit all the dubious inns, disgusting motels and round-abouts on the road - be it in Germany, Nigeria or Kazakhstan - the logistics did not matter. All that mattered was our mutual solipsism.

Our solipsism split in two shortly after France. Jerry 's came out on top.

I was left alone in the world again, with my own eye's projections of palm trees, cars or sedatives. I had stopped stealing. The only thing that set me free was the thought that we would see each other again next summer.

Then we postponed it for the next one.

And then for the one after the next one.

Then "the situation" began and the two ants remained locked separately in their jars.

I wrote to him kind-of letters, and he answered me with kind-of books. In our relationship, our passion for Plato prevailed. It had forever become a correspondence osmosis between two philosophers. I'm sure he'll be the next Hermann Hesse, and I'll be the next I-don't-know-who-fuck-with-books. Then historians will passionately review our letters - because, let's face it, historians are the most passionate of all people, the only ones who consider this life to be something wild and unsatisfied. And we will giggle and laugh from some grave - me in Bulgaria, he in Germany or vice versa. Logistics did not matter.

Or, what am I talking about - he will be cremated, because in Germany funerals are expensive. Even better. His dust will fly to me. Let's hope it won't confuse the grave. Well, no - he will feel by the breath of my bones who I am. I have the sweetest bones. That's what some existentialist told me, it seemed to be Albert. I still didn't understand what he meant. He and I didn't get along very well - he didn't like to steal. In general, he didn't like anything.

Well, that's enough about Finn. I love justice. What happened to Jerry? Nothing. I saw him one day at the Sistine Chapel. He smiled at me from above and waved. He had found some angel there. He was extremely happy, and blushed with shame.

Maria, that is to say, James, went to England and he sent me a greeting card from there. He'd married some Yorkshire goat and they drank tea every day, sharply at five. He'd cut off his dreads, put on glasses, and become a gentleman of class. Apparently that's all it takes to become a gentleman.

The Italian had become a birdhouse. But because he was a little confused, he rang like a clock every night at 12:35. The birds got scared and ran away from him, but finally they came back again – at the end of the day there was fresh water and two or three cookies inside. No one passed through this part of the forest anymore, because the tourists shit their pants. The birds there were ticking and speaking in Italian, and the worst thing was that they were shouting quotes from the bible about the apocalypse.

I remembered who was standing at my right that night — it was Pete. An Irishman, but a Northern Irishman, who played the ukulele.

Oh, someone rang the doorbell. I have to peel my ass off that couch. It must be a letter from Finn.

How he taught them, these letters, to climb up to the doorbell and press it, I don't know. And if you get this, what about sneaking through the crack in the door?

Yeah, the letter it was. Now I will sit in front of the fireplace and read it. Is it already 5? First I have to sit and have tea with my husband.

Cody's Half Book

After Granada, the whole world seems rotten - like after a holiday. The sky is all gloomy in Barcelona. I find the street of the homeless, and stop there for the evening. It is full of all kinds of characters, most of all harmless beggars or petty thieves. I lay my sleeping bag on the ground and wrap myself in it as much as I can, so that no one sees I am a girl. The next day, when I wake up, I go to the nearest park, Citadel. That's where I meet Cody. He is my age, twenty years old and has just left The United States. He was robbed a few nights ago while sleeping in the park. They took everything from him - the backpack, the passport, the wallet. I ask him what he intends to do and he tells me:

-Nothing. I will just keep on living.

-But won't you call the police?

-No.

Then we go for a walk. We get to the beach and spread there what we have – I, my scarf, and he- the only thing they didn't take - his clothes. I hand him my dress and my socks and ask him to keep them while I go for a swim. It's a wonderful day. The beach is overflowing with people. The water is warm and refreshing. When I come back from the sea some Czech women start arguing with us that we are stealing the shade of their umbrella, for which they have paid. We move a little to the left. We find a few mojitos left in the sand and finish them. I start laughing from happiness. After all, Barcelona is not that bad. Again, I seem to have everything I need - sunshine and a new friend. Cody jokes:

-Are you wasted?

We empty the mojitos to the bottom. It's time for lunch.

He takes me to a Hindu temple. Free food is served there once a day.

-I come here every day. I eat a huge portion of rice. That's all I need to survive.

In the evening he comes to sleep on the street with our small company of losers. Everyone accepts him very well - even the shoe thief who seems to have fallen in love with me.

-Mala suerte! -the woman who is my neighbor on a cardboard bed greets me.-Today it turned out that they've emptied the garbage bin in which we usually store our luggage. There was our whole cardboard house, and on top of that, your sleeping bag, which you had given me to keep.

She has a birthday tonight. They've brought a cake with a car picture from some children's movie. We divide it into as many parts as we can. The whole street rushes to celebrate with us - the limping dwarf, the Serbian musician, the divorced Spaniard whose wife took all his property, the gypsy family, and a few other colorful faces I see for the first time.

I'm so glad Cody is with me. He and I are the only ones in this late-night circus who are clowns by choice.

We both sit there on the ground and sink into some kind of sweet intoxication - the intoxication of hell and despair and chaos, but right there, at its very core, where we undoubtedly stand, there is something infinitely cozy, I don't know what, and aren't the people who've stopped searching the most enlightened in the world?... In the midst of this chaos of garbage, found mattresses and burning plastic, paradise will be born, Cody and I dream, and our rags, these are our wings. Everyone survives for himself. But sometimes on nights like this, when there are no stars and it's kind of very cold, then we all stand a little closer – all freaks without dreams, all travelers with too many of them, then everyone takes out what he has and here it is, the last piece of cake, divided in four, this is our communion.

Barcelona acquires another halo- the one of a holiday, which is not over yet. Cody sleeps next to me on the side of the street and I'm not the least afraid of pickpockets. They can only approach him, and he has nothing more to lose. I lend him a torn book I've found on the street. It tells of spiritual enlightenment and the key to immortality. I tell him:

-I found it like that, without the first hundred pages. I don't know who wrote it or what it's called, but it's amazing.

He laughs and replies:

-I do not believe you! You tore the first 100 pages because they contained the rest of the key, didn't you?

-That's right. If all the information is gathered in one place, you will know all the secrets of the universe, and if this falls into the wrong hands, it becomes dangerous.

The birthday girl and her husband go to bed without a house, and me without a sleeping bag. But none of us feels robbed tonight.

The next day is again a day for a walk. First, we have a picnic in the park with the food the social welfare service distributes every night on the street. We have everything - sandwiches, cakes, drinks. I ask Cody if he ever plans to return to the US.

-I don't have any plans for now. I bought a one-way ticket and that's it. You know, I didn't feel very well there... They wanted to take me to a psychiatric clinic because I felt a lot. I could feel the energy of each person, see how it flows through his body... Sometimes, if I touch the hand of another person,

I can tell exactly where the flow passes through the different points. It looks like a river, no, like streams, golden in color, rather sunny, but there is no such color in nature, the sun is the closest I can compare it to. Sometimes it moves very fast, and sometimes very slowly, as if it does not flow, but strains, and drops in level. Then I understand that the person is ill… But they started giving me pills. My parents thought I was crazy, even my sister thought I was crazy, everyone who knew me believed that I should be treated, that no such thing as streams flowing through the body exists.

I extend my arm to him. He closes his eyes and catches it where my veins stand out. He presses them with his fingers several times. Then he continues upwards, towards the bend of my elbow, stopping from time to time to press again.

Then he opens his eyes. I stare at him, waiting for him to say something. But Cody is silent.

-So?

-Nothing. I can't feel anything anymore…

The sun is shining in our sandwiches, but we are no longer hungry, in fact we've probably never been.

And I am thinking if there's anything more upsetting in this world than being blinded by force, let someone name it, because I can't think of it. But at the end of the day, Cody is very young, we are both very young, and life has yet to show us the flow.

We head to Gràcia .

"This is my neighborhood," Cody boasts. "Before I was robbed, I lived here in a hostel.

The color of wine hovers in the air. Our eyes are drinking. We don't talk.

-What sun? -I ask him.

-Sorry?

Someone thinks wine stains are ugly and pours a bucket of water on them. Then he throws soap on top and starts rubbing everything. I understand that the holiday is over and only dirty foam remains in its place.

-The sun you could see. Is it the sun behind the clouds or quite clear? Sun at sunrise or at sunset? I would really like to know.

-So would I. -laughs Cody with sadness.

Then we go silent again.

We reach Gaudi's park. We wait for everyone to leave and sneak in there just before they close. Then we hide somewhere behind the trees so that they don't kick us out, and as it gets dark we go on a journey.

We've landed on a fairy tale. The flower lizard has come to life, and the colorful columns are enchanted. We sit under them to have dinner. A large dog barks at us and then a lantern blinds our eyes. The guard is chasing us out, but we hide again.

We go to the top of the hill, from where you can see the whole city - a huge heart, pulsating in artificial lights.

You think that the heart gives life, but this heart is not like that. It will crush you and beat you as you walk towards it, intoxicated with the delusion that it is some kind of a dream sun. You believe that it will give you warmth, but you forget that not all hearts are warm, that there are those who need you just to keep pulsing and when they're done ripping every breath out of you, they will just spit you out and hang your glow on themselves in order to attract more deluded souls. And they will certainly come, because just like you, they will start thinking that the moon is a sun. And when they lose their last stream of brilliance, they will become moons themselves. But even though you know this, you are ready to try again, you are ready to engage in battle with this eternal murderer with the deaf hope that you will be different, that you will not have to steal light like the others. And even if you lose, which with no doubt will happen, you know that it had to happen, that you had to try first.

Somewhere there is our street, one of the many blood vessels, swollen and greedy for more blood; somewhere there our small group of losers is already lying on their cartons. They must have been spit out of the Heart for one reason or another, half chewed. They have become clots that everyone is afraid of. Sooner or later, however, they will be weaker than it. They will not be able to overcome the City, they will not be able to kill the Heart, because it is tough and relentless like any man-eating monster; sooner or later it will eliminate them to clean its vessels, and they will be thrown out of the system forever.

Then all the proper cells will rejoice because they will think they've gotten rid of the evil, not realizing that they are actually working for it, and all these clots are just symptoms, showing that the whole system is sick, thus being the only good. So they will appear again and again, the innumerable signs of this disease, they will appear until someone learns not how to kill them, but how to cure them.

I thought I was the one who could do this, but at one point I realized I could do nothing but get to know them. So if you ever see on the street some old man with a white beard covered with sand, with thick eyebrows and a shirt of coarse linen, and if this man does not breathe, do not think of him as one less evil, but as one more evil, think of him not as a clot thrown out of the system, but as a comet that broke away to give some distant sky a light, and above all, think of him as my friend, because it is quite possible that he once shared a piece of cake with me.

Such thoughts run through my head as I watch the big city. Suddenly Cody asks me:

-How did you decide to come to Spain?

-I knew I would die and my only salvation is the south.

Cody laughs with lips only. I see that they are cracked and blood-stained, just like the city.

-What about you, Cody?

-Me?… I just knew I would die.

It's time to go to bed. There's no point of going all the way back to our street. It would take us almost two hours.

He tells me to wait here because he's left his sleeping bag somewhere along the way in the park. When fifteen minutes pass, I start to worry. In half an hour I am paralyzed with fear. I'm alone in this park in the middle of the night, in one of the most dangerous cities in Europe, my phone battery is running out, and Cody is nowhere to be found. No point in searching, no point in shouting.

I'm starting to run. I am wandering through the paths. I'm trying to find my way out.

I finally find the park gate. I see the guard and ask him if a tall boy with brown eyes and chestnut curls has passed by.

The man shrugs. I say: "His face is very pale and his lips are cracked. He doesn't carry any objects, except, perhaps, a sleeping bag. " I say: "He is very young, only twenty, but he never intends to return home, in fact he no longer has a home and sometimes he sees the sun, right in the hands of the people…"

He replies sourly:

-No.

I feel the heart of Barcelona mercilessly beginning to chew me in. I am certainly His next victim. And His previous victim was a curly-haired young boy.

-Cody, Cody!

Nothing.

The city eats gluttonously, but quickly. One moment you're in terrible pain, but the next you're in pieces.

I spend the night on a street path wrapped in my new sleeping bag, which the shoe thief had given me. When the ugly face of darkness stops watching over me, I head back to our street.

One of the homeless people tells me that Cody passed by about two o'clock that night to look for me. I laugh at myself. During the day, Barcelona is a beach umbrella strewn with colors. And it wouldn't cross your mind that it eats people. My neighbor is coming. She has already made a new cardboard house. Her skirt flutters in the wind like a flamenco dancer's as she carries the last cardboard boxes. I don't remember seeing this skirt.

"It's new," her husband tells me. "I just found it in the trash and gave it to her. For her birthday!"

The birthday girl immediately drops the boxes and kisses him on the mouth. A toothless smile flashes across her face.

The street is almost empty today. Like every weekday, everyone goes downtown to earn a living. The shoe thief sells shoes, the musician plays his trumpet, and the limping dwarf begs.

"Farewell, we're leaving, too," the woman in the new skirt tells me, and her husband, caressing her shoulder, leads her down the street, pushing a cart full of cardboard.

I remain alone. I sit down at the place where I usually sleep and find the first hundred pages of my book that were missing tucked under a stone. Inside the cover it's written: "I hope you like it.-Cody."

I never see him again. He still has the second half of our book, my pair of socks and a few other small things that I had given him to keep safe. I probably hadn't found the most reliable person for the job. But in the end, isn't that life - you lose some things and gain others. For example, Cody lost his passport and money but received half a book and a pair of socks. I lost half a book and a pair of socks, but I got half a book and a friend. Not just any friend, but the man with the fewest possessions on Earth. And although the world is too big for us to meet again, it is certainly based on some kind of unshakable logic - because if a metropolis like Barcelona can gather all the deadbeats in one place, what is left for two losers who always win?

The Last Gospel

(written with love for every Jesus Christ)

Tonight, as with any other, three white candles are burning. They are placed in the throat of whiskey bottles and the melted wax, dried on the grooved surface of the glass, resembles a marvelous ice tower. Inside lives the spirit of all the people who once pressed their lips to its magical opening to taste the poison of fleeting happiness, and now lonely as a weathered memory, they kindle a fire at the top of their eternal prison. The wick- a black swan, bowing his graceful head, awaits his death in a lake of burning tears.

Oscar bends down from his hammock and lights a cigarette with the flame that illuminates my torn notebook. Here, long cigarette papers are revered. I've never seen bigger joints. They almost explode from weed, and even the most avid smokers find it difficult not to cough. Slowly the cigarette passes among all of us — Oscar, still quiet in the universal hammock perched between the trunks of two coconut palms; me, taking in the breath of the green herb as my thoughts linger in the fragrant cellar of my existence; Yannis and Johan, sitting next to me on the bamboo rug, interrupt their long game of chess; Masha, beautiful and idle, sitting on the low bench by the fence of palm leaves; Lach and Ferraro kneeling by the clay oven, from which hot smoke is rising. A few days ago, the boys built this hissing appliance resembling a magnificent turtle, and now they are making pizza for a second time. The first night, despite Lorenzo's best intentions, his Italian hands failed to roll out sand-repellent dough, and the newborn oven cried, rinsing its lungs over our warm dinner.

The second night, with a little less sand, the pizzas line up in circle like the joint. Small bites are taken by each of us until no more is left, and some of us collect with impatient fingers the vegetables fallen on the metal plate. Here the food is never enough to satiate you, but it's always shared. Only the fastest get utensils. I, who followed the Indian culture, enjoy the freedom to gather my food with hands, even in the evenings when we eat only rice or salad. My long red skirt, home to a farm for beige elephants, has seen a great deal of adventure this short month. The poor thing has traveled 3,000 kilometers from a North Indian market to the subtropical sands of the south, in whose suns it now lies. A napkin during the day and a blanket at night, it turned out to be the best 100 rupees spent in my life.

Our small circle is joined by other people - Pablo, the incorrigible Spaniard with skin that has absorbed the rays of coastal sunsets, and eyes that burst out with sparks toward every beautiful girl; Ati- the hyperactive Greek with whom our papaya breakfasts turn into papaya parties every morning; the absent-minded Adam-a Frenchman, floating behind round glasses, with hair protruding in all directions; Dennis, a nineteen-year-old German who learned how to take LSD from his tai chi teacher; Efe- a neighbor via country and palm hut; Basti, a compatriot of Dennis, with his muscular arms covered in tattoos and a bag full of psychedelic fluids; Neels, the boy from everywhere, with a smile reminiscent of something very familiar we all have lost with the first alluring whisper of adulthood.

Dinner is coming to an end. We are all half-hungry, enchanted and silent. Masha braids Ferraro's hair. He has unrealistically long dreads, swaying like satellites on his lungi-wrapped thighs. Here the boys are always barefoot, have crazy hairstyles, and rarely wear trousers. All of them are small Robinson Crusoes, shipwrecked in the ocean of the 21st century, where storms of loneliness never forgive; few discover the lonely island on which friendship exists.

Those friendships are not like the others. You can see it in the eyes of these happy boys. They never share their past. Instead, they draw their rough plans — to cross Rajasthan hitchhiking, perhaps next year; to swim from one beach to the other, maybe tomorrow, to go to Rainbow in Ethiopia, maybe the next full moon. But few of them live in the future. We never know how long we will stay here, or where we will be afterwards. When someone leaves, we send him away with a long hug. We know we will never see him again, because we are all children of the world, and the world is too big and too colorful to go back to our old dreams. We keep the rope of our friendship loose. Each of us can release it any time. It is like a nest in which we gather every night after a day full of multi-colored flights.

When we have food, we share our food. When the food is over, we share our silence. The rope that binds us is woven from this silence, and each holds one of its threads. Tonight, the threads shine like rays. The moon itself comes to us to compare his face with that of the sacred light flying straight from our open palms. We make a lasso and entangle its neck; we pull it to our small table. It is now a clairvoyant crystal in which the next huge joint is visible.

Dennis is the first to break the rope of our silence. He pulls out his drainpipe, painted with meaningless stripes and over-whelms the beach with the devastating sound of eternity.

No one can play like Dennis. He makes a great beatbox with his improvised didgeridoo. Our hearts race with Dennis', with his wild heart that will never stop beating on the wide roads of the world, spotless and magnificent like all his scattered dreams. Some people wait a lifetime for life to begin, and this boy has all the possible lives in him — that of the ocean and the sea turtles, that of the bamboo rug and that of the cunning gypsies, that of the Buddha, and especially that of the newborn ants, crawling all over the desolate land, which holds their thin bodies with open hands.

Neels sits at his djembe, fingers racing across the brown skin like the paws of a wild animal through the jungle. His soul remembers the leaps of the gazelle it once was, the last spasms of strong muscles, the scream of eternity foreshadowing the end, the unbearable bite of the tiger, pumping life out of the fragile skin of death. She also remembers the joy of the captured prey, the ecstasy of easy victory, pulsing in the blood like intoxicating fire, the grateful whimper of the little ones, looking forward to their sweet lunch. All the suffering of the world and all the happiness emanate from Neels's fingers, melt on the trembling back of the goat and water the roots of the mango tree, from which transparent eyes of children reincarnate.

Lisa emerges from somewhere. She sits in the hard sand with her back against the thin fence and embraces her planet-painted guitar. Her fingers caress the sleeping strings, occasionally raising their eyelids for a sleepy chord. I adore Lisa because the day before, despite my resistance, she took me to the sea in the middle of the night to show me the shining eyes of the plankton. It was as if all the fireflies in the world had learned to swim, and we, in our lonely paradise, plundered a handful of divine light. Then I promised myself that one day, when I forget the glow of the waves sparkling on my feet, I would meet Lisa again, by chance, in some concrete ocean and recognize her by the way she laughed yesterday in the cradle of the living stars.

We all know that tonight will never end — because Efe makes a tea of cinnamon and cardamom; because Denis is leaving tomorrow; because Masha is dancing, weaving her skirts with the shadows of palm leaves; because Adam, incredible and foolish, rolls a cigarette from a torn page of Mallarmé.

The crystal ball gravitating around our stone table looks impatiently at the silver-ornate sky. It is time to return to his eternal bride, eagerly awaiting the last diamond on her crown. We release the flaming lasso around the moon's neck. It inflates like a child's balloon, flies slowly into the sky and settles just above our heads, between the green irises of coconuts.

Out of the three white candles, only one remains burning. The spirit from the bottle has lost its hope and leaves the fire of the tower to smolder in the pouring darkness. And tonight, like any other, its prayer for salvation sinks into the throat of dreams. Masha squeezes the fallen stars out of her skirts with bare palms. Adam finishes his "formed calyxes balancing the future flask." Dennis collects the scattered fragments of eternity back in his gray pipe. And I am thinking that the most beautiful dance I'll ever see is that of the dying candle.

The flame colors Neels's calm face, on which a childish smile blossoms on its own. Blond dreads, scattered on the bamboo carpet like tentacles of a solar octopus, embracing in all directions the black bottoms of the sea, legs half-bent at the knees, surrounded by a green lungi; a white shirt darkened by the caresses of seashore sand dunes. I drop my pen and exclaim:

-Damn it, Neels, you look like Jesus!

Neels looks at me with his brilliant blue eyes, soaked with the rays of starry skies, which they close under every night, and with his crazy smile, revealing all his marvelously crooked teeth, he answers:

-I am Jesus.

The Answer

A Sunday like any other. I wake up in a sour mood. I drink coffee and prepare for the day. Sunday is my literature day. I leave it for reading. True, I don't read much, but at least I read something - poetry, a story, whatever. I browse the Internet and try to find new works. True, you can read from books. But the problem is that in my place the window is so small that almost no daylight enters. So if I read from a book, I will spoil my eyes. Which are spoiled anyway. In fact, I have a very high diopter. Sometimes I'm afraid I'll go blind. Of course, such fears may be unrealistic. But everyone has their own.

I'm afraid about a few more things. However, they are too realistic, judging by the circumstances. One of them is that I will never become a famous writer. Last year I was going to publish a book of short stories. I was so excited. In one week, I collected all the stories I had written, edited them, and sent them to two publishers. From the first I had no answer – not even a blunt "Thank you." That's what I expected. I wasn't upset. I had the second one left.

I received an annotation from them. Some writer with a page on Wikipedia had written that he liked my stories very much (in short, without all his snobbish roundabouts), but I had to edit here and there, fix this and that, write a few more to supplement the book. I was so happy! I jumped to the ceiling! I almost hit my head. I celebrated for a few days. That was a pure approval! I just had to remove this and that, add some shit here and there and I would have my own book of stories!

Every morning I woke up in my nasty studio, which was no longer that nasty. After all, this was the studio of a writer, god damn it! I was no longer bothered by the cockroaches, the broken mattress, the small window, or the stupid ceiling. I jumped out of bed in combat readiness, ran to the booth on the street, took a cup of nasty black coffee from the saleslady for the future writer, smashed a few cockroaches on my way back, and sat behind the computer.

Wasn't that a pleasure! I was spending all day rewriting my stories. I did not leave a single comma missing. I changed some stories completely. I cut out pages, five. I left nothing superfluous. Only the meat, no bones! After all, a real writer must be able to strike immediately, without verbosity.

When I wasn't editing, I wandered through the streets of Sofia. True, nasty streets. But a writer was wandering there! I was looking for stories. But, alas, there were no stories left. Good that I was manic-depressive. It helped me come up with two more. I was recreating, reediting, rearranging and voilà - the book, for a second time, was ready.

I sent the new version to the publisher. I did not receive any answer. One, two weeks... The studio began to shrink again. The window narrowed even more, as if it was taking diet pills. The coffee on the corner became even more bitter, unbearable. Only the cockroaches remained the same.

I decided to take the initiative. I wrote to the publisher - hello, I'm this and that, I've been waiting for an answer for two weeks now. I received it the same day. There would be no book. They've thought about it jolly well. They would rejoice in my future success and are looking forward to new proposals, but for the time being they do not give a fuck about me.

I didn't believe them. I thought- an e-mail sent by mistake. After all, that writer with a page in Wikipedia had written such a pretty, pretentious annotation about me... I just had to remove this and that, add some shit here and there and I would fly to the clouds with my new book.

I thought they were wrong. They will think for another day or two and realize what a huge mistake they have made. They will write me a second email. They will apologize to me. They will say - look, anonymous lady or sir, reviewing your stories we found that they have significant value and are unique to Bulgarian literature. We would be happy if you forgive our timely refusal and allow us to sign a contract this time… Or something like that. The details didn't matter.

Today I'm reading Mario Benedetti. I want to write a story again. I want to, but alas, there are no stories left. All turn out to be short, mediocre. My head will burst - not with ideas, but with boredom. Life is necessary for writing stories, life! Not some small room, in some nasty deadbeat town, in a nasty, boring Sunday. You have to travel. And I can't travel - I'm tied to my diploma, which I have to get. Oh, if only it wasn't for that diploma! If only didn't I have to crawl like a little animal to some pointless goal that I have to achieve in the name of someone else's happiness! I was fine with no money in Spain. I was fine, drunk and sick in Prague. I also had a good time in Portugal - lonely and arrogant with my funny suitors. Then there were stories.

There is nothing now. Only Mario Benedetti. He, bless him, lived in South America. I will go there, too - but when, I really don't know. Oh, how nice it would be in a year - in the summer! I would work like a donkey. Whatever it is! I'll become a man, if I have to. I will carry bricks, stones, I will live in a fucking basement, if I have to. But I will make a bunch of money and go to the end of the world. Then all the pathetic and disgusting publishing houses, all the nasty studios in Sofia, all the hateful diplomas, all pathetic years spent in darkness will wipe my ass, and this anonymous young lady will pile up stories after stories under the sizzling sun of Argentina. But alas, those publishers will not receive a sentence more. Because they will be broke, and I will be a millionaire.

I open my mail again. It's been a year since I was about to became a famous writer, and that snob with a page on Wikipedia had written such a pretty, pretentious annotation about me. And I keep thinking, they might have sent the last answer by mistake. Any moment now I will receive a letter from them, any moment now they will say that they have changed their minds. But the letter still doesn't come. It never comes, and my stories are covered with, look, that much dust.

The Shit

I had some interesting dreams tonight. At first, I dreamed of fucking a gypsy man, and a rat ran into his house. Still, I remember liking it. I was excited and almost finished. Then you showed up. We were standing somewhere in the sea and having underwater sex. My vagina was pressing against your cock and I was trying to rip out of you some emotion, some, if you will, manifestation of love intimacy. But you looked at me blankly, and when I tried to kiss you, you pursed your lips like a clam that doesn't want to open. So I tried for a long time to kiss you, but to no avail, until the alarm finally rang.

I went out and took bus number 11. I looked out for the ticket inspectors. I hadn't bought tickets in three months. I was once stopped and forced to pay a fine. The other times I was just sneaking out through the door before the fucking fat lady pigs had pressed their tits to my face. One of those got on today. I successfully escaped her and found myself at some nasty, soaked in cigarette smoke, vomit and remnants of masturbation stop on Slivnitsa Boulevard. Many times I had passed this stop by the bus and I was always puzzled how the hell there are people who go to this same fucking, nasty, dirty bus stop every morning and take in the fumes of dirty cars while smoking nasty, dirty cigarettes and sticking their fingers into their noses, the hardened mucus of which sticking to the nasty bench beneath them to make it even dirtier and wiping the shit they and their fellow citizens left the previous day with the jacket on their ass. And now I had to hang around next to the same lovely people, like a zombie waiting for the next bus. And I had to stick my finger into my nose, out of having nothing to do, wipe the dust with my pathetic ass and work passively but firmly for my lung cancer.

But I thought, is my life better than those of these fuckers here? After all, I live in the nasty capital, too! The stop I get on every day is pretty decent, compared to the other shit stops in Sofia, but on the other hand, my block is a stinky fly in the mouth of a dead rat, spat out a little earlier by a belching hyena. Even excluding the fact that the building has never been cleaned since its inception, the dust levels in the corridor are deadly, the old pensioner's floor stinks of their breath, soaked in drugs and tooth decay processes, and the walls look like they have been bombed during the second world war, there's one thing that still bothers me. I am not quite sure what to call this thing, since it is just, purely and simply, one big, brown, shiny piece of shit. Yes, that's right, a piece of shit.

This shit has been standing in front of the entrance of my building, not a meter away from the nasty decrepit door for almost a month now. I still clearly remember the first time I saw it. Since we live in a country where chaos likes to rage, we are used to seeing all sorts of absurdities, including owners who do not clean up after their dogs on the street. In this case, you are somehow ready to pass this disgusting little stool huddled next to the crack in the sidewalk almost without indignation, knowing that the animal, unlike us, cannot control its natural needs. With such a thought, I passed the shit. But after a second, recalling its size, I realized that it was created not by just any animal, but by the largest – the human.

This incomprehensible beast with a capital "H", present in the dictionary as a terrestrial mammalian creature, had stood in an opaque Sofia night under my window and sung with its hindquarters a long and emotional serenade. Whether he was a homeless man, a drunkard or a hooligan, I don't know. But what I do know, after my long scientific observation on the subject, is that shit doesn't decompose on cement.

Yes, it definitely changes its shape. First, as I mentioned, it was big, brown and shiny. A week later it snowed. I hoped, with all my childish naivety, that the snow would somehow evaporate it. But the snow melted and the shit didn't.

It waved at me again down there on the first of March, standing meekly and peacefully against the wall of the block. It had shrunk a little, but it was far from out of shape. On the contrary, it seemed to have tightened, gained more toughness and muscle mass after lifting weights of thick snow. It was no longer so shiny, on the contrary, it had faded a little, faded from loneliness.

Another week passed, but nothing more changed. The shit was still the same - light brown, round and stubborn, intending never to disappear.

I try not to see it. Every time I enter and leave the block, I deliberately turn my head in the other direction and whisk over to the "safe" part of the asphalt. But sometimes, for just a second, I catch it out with the corner of my eye, still standing there, my little friend, and he wishes me a pleasant day every morning on the way to the bus stop.

The old pensioners from the block, as I see, do not mind. After all, they haven't cleaned their building since the day they were born, which is almost a century! I thought- let's call a cleaning lady, at least one fucking time, to sweep that damn shit away once and for all! But then I gave up, for fuck's sake. Don't I have other problems? And in my head, as in everything around, there is one obscenely big shit.

I entered the next bus number 11. I bought a fucking ticket

this time. Some granny smiled at me. She must have thought me an exemplary citizen. It was March 8, and bouquets of flowers were being sold everywhere. It smelled of freshness, of hyacinths and tulips. But who knows why it still smelled like shit. We live here as if in the Middle Ages. The lack of canalization then created the most blossoming and unimaginable combinations of odors. Pee and homemade cakes, shit and fresh vegetables, sweat and silk fabrics. I was wondering what would happen if a boy, you for example, decided to bring me flowers. I would walk down to the entrance of the disgusting building, starting to smell, as I go down the stairs, of old age, I would come out of the door, perfumed and beautiful as an ancient muse, I would take the bouquet and blush from tenderness. Then you, also slightly blushing, would move back to make way for me and step on the shit.

What a date that would be! Then go and fuck me with romance. Go tell me I'm a beautiful princess and you are my knight on a white horse. No matter what dress I wear, no matter how green my eyes are, I still remain the girl who lives in the building with the shit.

Of course, the probability of you bringing me flowers is close to zero. They say that dreams always reflect reality. I still don't know what the pleasure of fucking a gypsy man in a dirty house should mean, but I certainly know what it means to fuck with you while you don't open your mouth. My love, I have no reason to deceive myself; I've long realized that you don't give a single fuck about me. Your dick has long been in god knows how many vaginas since the day we met and none of them has been mine, not even in your dreams.

I finally arrived for class. I had Russian and I wanted to sit in the first row, next to Miss "Fat Grumpy Face", because if I sat in the back, I wouldn't see the board well. I didn't know her, but I kindly asked if it was fine to sit next to her. She just muttered something incomprehensible. She seemed to make a sour face. But I thought, "I'm imagining it. Why would this pimple monster mind somebody paying a little attention to her?"

Then, when the break came, she got up and, without saying a word, began to pack. She moved to another desk. This situation was so absurd that it didn't even leave me space to take offense. Why the hell would some she-elephant who doesn't even know me move demonstratively away from me!? To show her that I was a well-behaved lady with high self-esteem, I even offered to help her move by handing her the bag, to which she, again without saying a word, responded with a sour snort.

I thought, "Is there anything wrong with me, damn it? I'm supposed to behave and look nice. Or maybe I smell like something, for fuck's sake? No! Even if I live in the building with the shit, I'm still cleaning mine. What is it, then? "

I never understood. I decided not to pay too much attention to the situation. There are too many asses in this world.

However, I told the story to Gloria that evening. She was waiting for me at the restaurant to celebrate International Women's Day. I was in a terrible mood. Shortly before that, I got lost looking for The Barn. Because its location was kept secret and was never on the maps, I wandered for half an hour on "September 6" St. like a decapitated hen. Did I not hate that drunkard's hole with all my guts, did I not despise it…? But I had to find my earring that I had lost some time ago. That place was my last hope.

The bartender calmly and slowly poured coke into two glasses. I had the feeling that this was going on forever. When she finished, she didn't pay any attention to me either. So I decided to take the matter into my own hands, and although I was overheated with irritation, I asked her politely:

-Excuse me, miss, have you happened to find a moon-shaped earring here?

The wrinkled bitch grinned amusedly and responded with a determined:

-No.

That's why I had stormed into the restaurant. The good thing is at least I looked sexy. I was wearing a black tank top and a black bra with gold pieces on top. I had decided that this bra was for show only, and it was not at all obvious that it was not part of the tank top. By the way, I didn't admit it, but I was upset about something else. My ex never congratulated me on March 8th. Yes, an ex, but we still remained friends. Friends, with the possibility of a desperate fuck.

It's been almost six months since I've slept with somebody. Not that there were no opportunities, I'm just kind of tired. I want to meet someone special, not just some loser - like you or my ex. I want real love. Fuck, that's all I want.

Gloria was the only person who gave me a flower. We drank a glass of wine and had fun. As always, we started talking about fucking. I told her about my dream with you and how you didn't want to open your mouth.

-This means that the drug addict doesn't like me, does it?

We call you "the drug addict" to make it easier. Otherwise, I always fall into a kind of paranoia that you will appear from somewhere and you will understand that we are talking about you.

-Mmm. -she said with friendly concern.

Then we went to a gay club. We had planned to do this a long time ago so that men would not try to fuck us. That was the most disgusting thing of all- some horny pig approaching you and starting to pull his stupid jokes.

We started dancing. I didn't feel like going home at all tonight, and not because it was a lot of fun. The music was mediocre, nothing special. It was just kind of repulsive to see my little friend so soon again. Yes, although it was only for a moment a day, I had developed some aversion to even entering and exiting the block. It was as if I always suffered a mild nervous breakdown before that, as if I was expecting something bad to happen to me. Of course, nothing bad was ever happening, but something fierce and quiet was constantly protesting inside of me. Not because of the shit itself, but because of the whole disgusting situation. Because my neighbors would rather sniff it than get this thing out of here.

Meanwhile, some man in high heels passed by us and raised his glass for cheers. We said we were still waiting for the waiter. He came up to me, put his hand on my shoulder, and gracefully stated: "Honey, never ever wait for a man, especially if he's a faggot."

A Letter to Brodsky Because Santa Claus Doesn't Answer

Joseph, precious,

First, I'd like to mention that our entire acquaintance is a result of a terrible tangle of misunderstandings.

Its first knot tangled up on a gloomy afternoon at high school, on a bench. If I had followed it, you would have saved at least seven or eight years of my life, because I, like you, wanted to leave school at 15. Alas, no one told you there that the Nobel Prize winners in literature did that. On the contrary, they argued that studying was the path to success and non-studying was the complete and final collapse. Why I'm telling you- you probably already know…

You must have been told that you will be dragged through dirty factories until one day you get thrown in prison - this is the future of everyone who leaves school at 15, right? And they were right, мой мальчик. They were right. But they forgot to mention that this would give you soil rich enough for all the flowers of genius to blossom. And therefore, the next great writer will be you.

But let's go back to that horrible yard, where I had the misfortune to spend every 20-minute "break" for 5 years of my life. There I had made some friends who clucked around me like chickens every time they saw me, and I, in turn, did the same to fit into the henhouse. Why am I telling you? You probably already know that, too...

Anyway. One day one of them, the tallest and most educated hen of all, mentioned your name. I don't remember the reason, or the context that surrounded this island with glowing neon then - "Brodsky". I only remember that then I really wanted to swim to it. Someone seemed to have stamped your name on the clavicle of my shoulder, and since then it has stood there as something way familiar but unexplored.

"What will this Brodsky be like?" -I thought. This must be what people call love at first sight. Or in this case, from the first letter.

I guess I liked it because it reminded me of a "brodyaga"- a tramp in my language. And I'm like that myself, my darling. I know what you're going to say now. I know exactly what you are going to say! "Content, not form..."

Oh, don't pretend to be innocent, you're exactly the same. You fell in love with me only because of the color of my eyes, without knowing me at all.

I came home with a nagging feeling in my chest. My breath was heavy and creaked like ice. I was lying on my orange blanket in the cold November afternoon and I thought to myself, "I have to have him!"

I ordered you the same day. "Lonely journeys," was written on your forehead. They handed you to me, wrapped like a newborn in several fluffy sheets. I undressed you quickly and put you on the shelf above my bed.

The second knot was a walk in Petersburg. I thought back then how nice would it be to find some special fella – some blond St. Petersburgian. How would we live with him in a cardboard crate with beautiful facades in the front, how would we watch the snowflakes melt, caught by the wet tongue of the window and walk hand in hand when it warms up and when it doesn't. We would cross the Neva with large umbrellas, baptize the lanterns with kisses, and walk boldly like crusaders until we found ourselves in front of the sinister teeth of the Cross.

Oh, how nice would it be then! But I was alone in Petersburg -- if we don't count my special fella at the time - a colorful but headless Muscovite who had come to visit me for a day. The rest of the time I went on pilgrimage to the Holy

Places, loaded with only a headscarf, a short-sighted camera in the eye of my phone, and a few verses in my head. First, I bowed to Dostoevsky, then to Pushkin, Nabokov, and finally to Aunty Annie. Your Annie- the lady with the notebooks from the third floor.

That's when fate kicked me in the ass again, manifesting via the poke of a security guard who really wanted me to see your office. I have no idea what this insistent hospitality was about. Perhaps he saw my confused face wandering through the floors, noticed my presence by my strong, I suppose even ridiculous-to-you language snobs of the mainland, accent, and felt sorry for my ignorance, which he had to immediately wipe out with an anti-idiot eraser.

This reminded me of another episode in my life that was about to happen a little later - in a hostel in Bratislava. But as you and I know, life is not a chronology of before and after, but a constant mess of memories. So don't be surprised at me remembering something that was about to happen - there in your world such things happen all the time. There was a Russian in this hostel, probably also from Petersburg, who tugged me at my sleeve with insistent friendliness when he saw me munching on a piece of food left in the common room. You already know me to the point of pain, dear Bro, so you know that one of my most distinctive features is my systematic laziness, and you wouldn't be surprised if you see me stirring up some spaghetti left to chance instead of going to the store; especially on some terrible night. But the Russian, like most people in his place, took my act of food recycling as a proof of extreme poverty and almost forced my hands to grasp some kind of biscotti- yes, exactly. Some funny box of biscotti.

-"Vkusno." –He pronounced slowly to explain his gesture of mercy, and he even made a sign with hand that this is for eating.

-No, no! - I answered

But he kept repeating: "Vkusno, vkusno…"

I had no choice but to accept my new dessert. With these biscotti in backpack and a few bags of lousy tea, I was able to cross the world and even more.

It's exactly how it seemed to me when the security guard was pushing your paper dough cabinet into my hands, but instead of "Tasty, tasty", he was repeating "Brodsky, Brodsky…"

I vaguely remembered hearing that name before. Your stamped island appeared on the collarbone of my shoulder like a déjà vu. But then it brightened again. I took a quick look at both the box and the biscotti. The guard pulled out his idiot eraser again and began rubbing the flat surface of my forehead.

-This is Brodsky. - he said.- Our writer Joseph Brodsky.

-Who?- I replied

He all of a sudden got furious and started to rub even harder as my forehead was slowly bruising.

-Don't you know Joseph Brodsky? Our writer Joseph Brodsky? The one who emigrated to America because he was expelled from the Soviet Union? The same one who won the Nobel Prize for Literature in '87?

Nope. I don't think I do. If he had said, "The one who dropped out of school at 15 because he was bored," maybe I would.

The third node was some strange and curious chain of circumstances named "coronavirus". I will not explain too much, as not to bore you. I will just tell you that was a blissful and happy time when everybody stayed at home reading a lot of books. At some point that time I looked at the shelf above my bed. And I read the name of some "Joseph Brodsky".

Who will that one be… Oh, no, no, no, wait a minute! I've been a guest of his. After all, that eraser had not been useless. I rubbed my forehead - it still hurt.

Since then, you and I became inseparable. I had wet dreams with you. Don't laugh at me, because you know very well what I'm talking about. Or was it not you who walked Horace's shadow between a bed and a radiator?

Well, I dreamed of other things, too. I will paraphrase one of your quotes and say that there is nothing more boring than someone else's dream, unless there are scenes of sexual acts in it and unless they are with you. Otherwise, they can take you out of the shell with jealousy. This is how all sea snails died, listening to their significant other talk about some crab or some coral with obscene shapes.

I can forgive you only in a single case, and that is if the object of your passions has been dead for 2,000 years, and only if he was a man. If possible, a writer. Only then can I understand your interest in the forms; in the forms of speech, I mean. Because it has long been clear that we writers fall in love just with that. I tend to make only one exception for gender and that is Sappho – we've all had erotic dreams with her. And I'm trying to remove double standards from my value system.

I will divide my letter into parts of arranged biscotti, as you do in your essays. I hope it'll be easier for you to eat it.

I

I walk to your bathroom without clothes and I ask you to give me a towel. I secretly hope you don't give it to me.

You hand me my orange towel, orange again.

What does that mean, Joseph? Does that mean you don't want to read my letter? I will be very offended if you don't. I, unlike you, am very sensitive. And the secret of long life is not to take offense. So if you want to kill me - go ahead - stop reading!

It can, of course, mean you have a wife. So my dream has gravitated between '90-'96. But don't you let it bother you, if that's the case. I came out of my shell a long time ago and I still seem to be alive.

I want to assure you that our love is mutual. Mine took a little longer to be born, but it's already a fact. You fell in love with me back when we were in Venice, and my greenish-brown eyes sparkled in the windows of the water. This woman who stole them from me, she deceived you - she was just a pale reflection of my Self. She wanted to do this to you - she wanted to make you fall in love by stealing me from the future. What a fortune, what a luck that you fell in love only with my eyes then, and not with her whole face. So our love has remained pure to this very day. One of the knots unraveled. When will we sew a sweater? When will I pull you out of there? Grab the thread of the cloth one evening as I toss it into the sky. I know gravity is in the opposite direction there, but try to push yourself towards me. I will close the door of my balcony so that the warm air does not escape, I will cut the thread and I will plant your feet with two nails - ghosts do not feel pain, right? So you will stand on my terrace like a helium balloon, and I will come to inflate you every day so that you don't disappear.

You ask me what we will do all this time. Don't be afraid. I have prepared a long and emotionally wasteful program for you. It involves drinking a lot of coffee. You like coffee?

I make Turkish coffee in pots, and I have a real espresso machine. One cup of espresso in the morning, two coffee pots for lunch, and in the evening…in the evening whatever you want, darling, we can have it both together. Sometimes I wonder which of us is more of a corpse. This devil's liquid is also the only support that keeps the hut of my body from collapsing. If one day I spew you with straws - don't be afraid - it's from the roof.

We will sit on my bed – I, like a hut of wheat sticks, you like a balloon, woven in a particularly unimaginable way which will look like a basket, and we will read what you like to read.

I looked through your list of books and saw nothing to excite me, but if you insist that much, you can recite Horace to me. What if, after all, I fell in love with him, what if we end up making some mutual dream, the three of us together?

Then you will give me a chance - I know that you hate Russian literature, because it reminds you of your dark past, but without Yesenin you are going nowhere. And if I really want to torture you, I can take out Mayakovsky - you love sadomasochistic performances sometimes, don't you?

Otherwise, it gets boring.

II

A demon visits me in my bed and assures me that he must take the place of my soul if I want to keep it clean. Otherwise, he will move in with it and stain it. That's why he has to get it out right away. He must immediately settle in my body.

Oh, these erotic dreams, how quickly do they get replaced by nightmares! This must have been your '90-'96 wife. Tell her to leave me alone. I will not let her love you through me.

Good thing I woke up on time! You pushed me slightly with the end of your essay and thus saved me from getting possessed.

It's such a pity you can't kiss me because your lips have evaporated. You take one of your books, scrape a few letters out of it, and stick them to my mouth.

Nipple - this time I dream of a nipple. The shot is vague, obscure and composed with red back-lighting like a porn movie from the 90's. I manage to distinguish a woman's nipple. I reach for it with my lips. Then I startle. No, this is not Sappho. This is a woman I certainly don't like.

How many more faces, shapes, and body parts will she acquire to push her ass between us in bed?

Tell her to leave! What's her name? Maria? All of them are named Maria.

Maria, please!

The light turns off.

III

I am sitting on the beach in Petersburg. I'm alone. There are children's goodies all around me- all kinds of toys, candies, lollipops, plastic in various pink shapes, everything that can lead the potential owner to hysteria, and his potential parent to even more potential bankruptcy.

There are also the irrevocable kissing couples - not like you and me, but simple, uneducated hens with their even simpler roosters. They have never read Yesenin, heard of Horace, or thought of you in three dimensions. This is not Dostoevsky's Petersburg, but the Petersburg of… you name it, some contemporary writer that none of us reads.

Tasteless, awkward, full of unraveled adventures, called by chance St. Petersburg. I look for the rescue signs. But there are no balloons around me other than those with the faces of characters from Frozen. (I'll tell you later.)

They sold Petersburg for a few pieces of silver. Yes, it could get worse, dear Yoska. Where are you, aren't you in my bag like at any other time?

No, you're not there either.

A child whispers the answer to the knotty riddle. You are that sand castle over there. Yes, Yoska, it's you! How could I not remember it before!

IV

I walk the streets of Petersburg and look for you. Hasn't the

Venetian water already come? How much longer does it need to flow into the Neva? Can't someone lightly shake the globe? Can't a child with a plastic shovel push the water from one channel to the other? Then I will be satisfied.

But a startling thought strikes me. It strikes me just as I ruffle my bun, walking towards one of the river's lions. I stop next to him and growl fiercely.

The lion looks at me without any fuss. Since the time of Dostoevsky, he has been accustomed to people growling at him. He doesn't even say to himself: "Look at this mortal, how dare she growl at me! I'm a lion, hey! No one can growl louder. " He doesn't even want to bite me. I am not worthy of such an effort. To bite me! Alexander Ist has stroked his mane with the tip of his golden ring, and some savage, this girl, will growl at him!

I lean on the lion and start crying. You did not live in Petersburg, Joseph!

V

We live in two parallel universes. One is called Petersburg and the other, Leningrad. Some mortal might confuse them. He may decide that it is the same place on the map. But we both know that's not the case. We know that names have changed the whole structure of the living organism. They have shuffled its molecules, and once you've shuffled its molecules, you've shuffled its little soul. The wind becomes a branch, the river becomes a cloud, and the nose becomes a trash can with one push of the button. Then why are we surprised that the city has been replaced?

Someone has shaken the globe, shaken all the cities in the world, and although a hundred years have passed, it is still dizzy. It's all upside down. After a while, I wouldn't be surprised to see penguins torn to bits by jaguars.

A thick waterproof jacket bruises my shoulder. I'm getting ready to shout, "Hey, you bastard, stop at least to say sorry!"

But someone puts a hand on my lips. Or rather a paw. The lion woke up and looked at his watch.

"There's no point in being grumpy at him," he tells me. "He's from Leningrad."

Wow, he's right. The meridians are confused again. They've unintentionally hit me with a man from another city.

The belly of the globe is bloated with several magnetic storms and a jug of fuel oil. All the continents are squeezed in like potatoes in an old sack, and no one wants to get out. Africa kicks with its feet on the nose of Asia, Asia screams and pulls Europe by the hair. We'll all throw up in a little while.

I look at the man again. Even if I called him, he wouldn't answer. But I want to continue this game a little longer. I want to see who he is.

I sneak behind the bridge. He stops in front of a bakery,

picks up two buns, and continues. Someone help, please!

The lion jumps and stands in front of him. The man bends down to stroke him. Brodsky!

This is you, Brodsky himself! I remember when you bought this coat in Venice. You couldn't wait to buy it, so you put it on a little earlier. Underneath, you're wearing your prison uniform. They let you take a walk while you were still asleep. No wonder you don't pay attention to where you are going.

The planet belched. All the meridians came into place. Several heads hit the wall from the quick rebound of its elastic soles.

VI

The knot, instead of unraveling, became even larger. Now the lousy years have intervened.

One day as I was walking with you hand in hand on the street someone asked me who that was. "My husband."- I answered.

-You don't have a husband.- the boy replied, a little disappointed.

-I do!

-Since when?

-Since 1996.

-Wait, what? Which year you were born?

-97.

He laughed. Apparently, he thought it was a joke.

Oh, only if he knew that my sense of humor is like Fontanka in December - frozen from the navel to the pants, and lower you don't even want to go.

Do you remember, Brody? You got a little offended back then. This probably reminded you that our age difference is too big. Minus one year.

Some joke for accountants - you die in 1996, I am born in 1997. You die on the 28th of January, I was born on the 27th.

The numbers have gone wild with the talent of an artist this time. So why should they paint such strange pictures? A year later or a day earlier, our souls would have kissed before they passed each other in the afterlife - me downwards, you upwards.

VII

Someone found, discarded at the sea, several fishing nets, torn and tangled like our yarn.

At that very moment, your castle collapsed and turned into sand, which the sea took away. One of its grains flew to the bottom because it wanted to reach another. One day, after another 2000 years, a child will play on the beach and bring us together.

VIII

You wrote to Horace in '95. It turns out that this was your death letter. How did you know when you were going to die? Was this on purpose?

It must have been on purpose, since you made me exactly minus one year younger than you.

I know it's obscene to read other people's correspondence. But I couldn't help it. I also read your letter to Marcus Aurelius- I admit that I did not expect your hyperborean self-absorption to reach the North Pole, no matter how often we hang out on the iceberg of misanthropy.

Is it that you say on the day we die, we lose only one thing and that is the day itself? Or rather the rest of the day.

Didn't it occur to you that you lose me?

IX

Look at my body. You will see that only a few nerves, as entan- gled as an old fishing net, remain.

Someone has thrown my body in the sun. He dried it well like a copper pear, then cleaned everything unnecessary, as fruits are cleaned for tea, and finally left the nerves only. Those useless-to-anyone speechless nerves.

These nerves are walking now through Petersburg's wind, biting each of their tips with its white teeth. These nerves greet you and these nerves pass you in the box office queue.

The whole mystery is how are they alive. And yet they live, smoke cigarettes, go collecting snails to save them from cars in the rain, drink whiskey, read Simone de Beauvoir, fall in love, break, and tie themselves again like thin threads re-knotted.

There are more and more knots each day, and the threads become thinner and thinner. It would be a real miracle to unravel them. One day someone will come here and say, "Ew! This mess of yarns is only for the trash!" And just like that he will throw me into the sea.

Along with all my stories. Along with all my notebooks.

X

Did you find me, Joseph? Or will I still have to look for myself?

Not to Run the Hot Water

Today I walked around Hackney to see the old house. I was 15 when I first got there. And the financial crisis had begun about four years earlier. My father, who was selling real estate at the time, couldn't make a penny more. Shortly after the crisis began, he went to prison for a year - for some nonsense, but enough to make my mother shed tears all day long, and my relatives to look at me with undisguised pity, avoiding the word "prison" as if it were a dirty word such as "pussy", "ass", "fucking", and I'm some little kid who neither suspects their meaning nor shall ever understand it. For my part, I thought there were things worse than having your father in "that place" – like your mother being on the edge of suicide, nasty classmates, and visiting aunts who underestimate your intellectual capacity.

For three years we drove on savings and loans from the neighbors. My father was released from prison and started a new business, this time selling antiques, but as you can guess, he wasn't doing very well either. In the meantime, my parents got divorced. My mother, intending to treat her worn-out nervous system, had begun to read all those books about positive thinking and was soaking up the drops of the latest wave of feminism with every pore of her skin. I remember her one day proudly waving a document at my face, certifying her new or rather old family name and almost forcibly making me congratulate her on her success. Then she removed the plate with the family name "Zhelyazkovi" from the bell of our apartment and put a new one on which in large block letters was written "KOLEVI", forgetting that I still bore my father's surname.

I had already left the small town and lived in an apartment in Plovdiv. Somewhere then, I was in the eighth grade, my mother found a job in England. I still remember the noise of her car from the small blue street when she left for the first time. It was a bright autumn after-school afternoon. The Plovdiv summer was still burning. The cobblestones rattled. I ran to the terrace, and she was gone.

She first spent a year in Colchester, a caretaker in some retirement home. Then she moved to London. She started working as a housekeeper for a Bulgarian, called Damian. He was a terrible man - racist, stingy, arrogant, but my mother had no choice - she had to take care of me somehow. I was in an English high school in Bulgaria and had no greater dream than to see the city of the queen. My mother somehow managed to persuade Damian to receive me in his house, even if only for a while. I arrived one gloomy afternoon; summer vacation had just begun. Damian, by the way, was not as rude to me as to my mother. The old miser clearly saw in me some last chance to pass on his philosophy of life to the younger generation. It included aversion to everything that existed and a lot of alcohol. He opened a bottle of wine on the table for me and began to pour it. It was, of course, the cheapest wine, but he didn't fail to point out that he himself had bought it to treat his guest.

My mother had lost weight. There was no sign of her full, authoritative thighs, which seemed to give orders at home on their own. Her expensive leather skirts from boutiques had not adorned her for a long time. In their place there were only tracksuits and jeans, and her highheels had long been gathering dust in the old closets of our apartment. Something powerful, confident, was still present in her manners, but now some fear was creeping in.

One night I took a bath. I could only dream of such thing in Bulgaria. I thought "a bathtub - this is what happiness and wealth is. This is the only way to know if you've arranged your life or not- you have a house or an apartment with a bathtub!" When I went out, my mother started a scandal with me in the corridor because of Damian's house rules - her daughter could not waste hot water in his house. With that, my happy summer in London was over. It looked happy only from the pictures of Madame Tussauds, Big Ben and all that similar London nonsense. The rest of the time I wondered how to escape from the house, from Damian and from my mother, whose guts, as you can guess, I hated --naively, but painfully and sincerely, as only a daughter can hate.

So, I was a typical example of a depressed teenager going through an existential crisis. With divorced parents, one abroad and the other, as the evil tongues would say, "with a dubious record," moving four times in two and a half years, I had no choice but to pig out on cheesecake, and fill up the bath one last time, being careful not to accidentally turn on the hot water.

Only those who have hated their mothers know that then you hate yourself and the whole fucking world, too, even in the summer - that disgusting, lonely, cheesecake London summer. And if you're a teen with suicidal tendencies, this aggression must get released somewhere. If you are a boy, by beating someone, and if you are a girl, as in my pathetic and ridiculous case, by starting to look for trouble falling in love with someone almost twice your age.

Who knows why in my case that was some snotty, blue-eyed Polish fuck. His name was Michał. or some other similar Polish bullshit, but he introduced himself to everyone as

Michael — whether because he wanted to break with his emigrant past or because the English were too dumb to remember anything else — I don't know. But in any case, I started calling him that.

He worked in the park as a boatman. I am not sure there was a name for his profession, so I decided to call it that. He was standing in some booth by the lake, quite reminiscent of an eco-toilet with a window on the side, and if someone wanted to take a boat ride (which very rarely happened) he would step out and sell him a ticket. Then he untied the boat from the ramshackle pier, explained how to use it, and returned to the "toilet." He had tousled hair and looked like a tramp. But that, of course, didn't matter to me at all because I was in love! This was my second big love for this year. The first one, which ended painfully and tragically, was with some twelfth-grader, Kiko, on my departure to London. Although it had lasted only half the summer, I did not fail to record it in my diary as "fatal". I saw my mother as the monster that took away the love of my life, and that summer as its end. Kiko was, after all, the first boy I'd ever been on a date with. And yet, if you noticed, only a single one. He took me to some hill, taught me how to smoke and sent me home. Of course, we couldn't even talk about sex. I had not even been kissed yet.

Ever since I discovered my new great love, I started taking walks in the park absolutely every day. I told my mother and

Damian I was jogging. The old sucker looked at me from under his eyebrows and muttered: "Don't you even think of speaking to black monkeys or Indians." I flew like a bird from a cage, ran down the street, rounded the corner at the Lariston Pub, and a little further down, behind the roundabout, ran through the majestic dark blue gates, with "Victoria Park" written above in golden letters. There it is, after the second alley, the lake. All that time I was thinking how I would start a conversation with Michael, what I was going to tell him. Approaching the shore where the small boats were, saying "hello" to the ducks and the geese, I saw the Pole standing behind the small funny window, and my heart began to beat in my heels. "Now what?"

-Hello Michael!

-Oh, Nina!

-How are you?

-I'm ok. Want to take a boat ride?

-Oh, no. I just … went for a walk. I accidentally thought of you and decided to stop by.

-All right. Just a moment, I think these people… Do you want two tickets, miss?

The other times I went to the park, I didn't even have the courage to talk to him. I must have been circling the lake about ten times each day, forcing myself to meet him, but never succeeding. Finally, I sat behind a tree, flushed with shame, and said to myself, "You fool, you idiot… What's so hard about it? Is it so difficult to say just one "hello"??"

Two months passed this way. The weather over London was still fucked up, my mother and I were still fighting. Damian continued to buy the cheapest wine, and I continued to not use the bathtub. Michael probably didn't remember me anymore.

One day, just before I was about to leave, I thought, "Now or never." What would I lose anyway!? I had to meet him, I thought. After all, everything in this world boils down to honor and dignity, and what kind of dignity do you have if you are afraid to talk to the one person you can't stop thinking of every single day of your fucking life?

I ran to the park, full of shame and anxiety. I approached the lake, ready to fly full speed in the opposite direction, but I did not give up. I kept on saying to myself, "You can do it. It's now or never!"

The Pole was waist-deep in dirty water. He wore a green rubber jumpsuit and arranged the boats in their places. It was about five-thirty in the afternoon. The sun was almost visible that day. It wasn't so windy, either. I waved at him from the shore. He saw me and replied with the same gesture. He even seemed to be smiling at me. This encouraged me and I sat on a bench by the shore, waiting for him. An obviously older girl appeared from somewhere and shouted at him that when he was finished with the boats, he was free to go. Then she came up to me. We were sitting like that, next to each other in stillness, both silently watching the boatman's abrupt movements. At one point she unexpectedly looked at me and with a cheeky, on-the-verge-of-a cackle smile asked: "You like Michael, don't you?"

There was so much nasty self-complacency on those lips that I wanted to jump right into the lake. She looked exactly like some red, large-nostril snake ready to devour her pray. Embarrassed and upset, I didn't have a fucking clue what to answer to that little rattling remark. I only managed to mumble: "No, I…how…" And then, deciding not to give up without a fight, I added with false confidence "Well, Michael and I are friends! Just friends… And what's wrong with saying hello to a friend?"

This time she right away snorted with her vile snout. I clearly felt as if I were sinking into the Pole's lake, without a green rubber jumpsuit.

I waited for Michael until it got completely dark. Finally, he came out of the lake in his muddy green rubber jumpsuit and looked at me in surprise. He hadn't even expected me to still be there! But I spoke out, half-timidly, half-excitedly: "Since you've finished work, do you want to take a walk, here in the park, or somewhere else? I mean, if you feel like walking…"

He frowned, somewhat annoyed, and muttered, "It's too late. And I'm all dirty, I have to go home and change. Maybe some other time." I, stepping over the edge of my girlish shyness, replied with some quiet, crabby "Good." I gave him a second to ask for my phone, and when time ran out I rushed home with all my might, in competition with the blush on my cheeks.

I never saw Michael again. The summer was over and I returned to Bulgaria. I did not return to London for five years. My mother was still there. She had already moved to another neighborhood, Chiswick. She now had a good job near Green Park, and she made some good money. But she always dreamed of returning to Bulgaria. She was always dreaming, and something was always popping out. Sometimes she had to spend money on repairs, sometimes on my university, sometimes on something else. And so the years went by.

My father, like me, kept on moving. How many cities did he change, how many nameless villages did he not travel through! He was still buying and selling antiques. What a job! He was already 65. But he didn't rest. He carried everything from buckles to scimitars through dusty country squares of big blue mountains. If someone asked me where I was from, I no longer knew what to answer. I felt, like those sacks of antiques, as if someone had dragged me all around the world.

Damian had died. The house was still the same, only a little neglected. The white walls were cracked and the plaster had begun to fall. It was obvious that no one had lived there for a long time. Here, at last, Damian's wish had come true: "Not to run the hot water."

And I'll admit it, I felt a little sad for this arrogant fucker. I was sad that no one here had left a message. No one would look at this unfortunate little house except to say to themselves: "Poof, what a dump this house is around the other shiny facades lined up like soldiers!"

Only the door was still pure blue. Blue as that afternoon, when I rushed to the park with my last hopes. The handle was still trembling from my fifteen-year-old, ripe dreams, from my excitement on the first entry, from saying goodbye on a vague, rainy afternoon, with no idea that I would never step through that threshold again. How many memories can a door hold? How many ghosts, how many unrequited passions! In my opinion, Damian's ghost was hidden in the doorknob. If you just touch it, it would bite you with its small metal beak and it would make you step back.

Everyone is afraid of abandoned houses, and I am just the opposite. Is there anything better than the past? It's over, but everything looks different, just a little more beautiful.

I went for a beer at the old Lariston. This is where I scribbled that story.

And the lake?

Yes, you're right! Naturally, I passed it by. No boats left.

Mid-August Semi-Storm

Evgeni started the car.

-Are you cold?-he asked. -I can give you socks and slippers.

-Yes.- Natasha replied. -My feet are dripping wet.

She had been waiting for Dima on a park bench for almost an hour when a great storm raged over Moscow. Out of nowhere, the trees twisted branches, the rain flooded the streets, and seconds later a terrible hail poured down. And it was only mid-August.

Natasha ran down the alley, soaked to the bone, when she saw Evgeni. She no longer remembered what he asked her or what she asked him, but they ran together, sheltering under his black umbrella.

-You can hold my hand.-he said, and Natasha did. Not because she wanted to flirt, but because it was far more comfortable to take shelter under an umbrella. At first opportunity, she hurried to clarify that she had a boyfriend so as not to leave the gentleman with the wrong impression. But such a river had formed at their feet that when he offered to lift her up her in his arms, she agreed, and so he carried her almost to the door of his car.

-So… here are the slippers! I hope you are not very cold. What was your name again?

-Natasha.

-And mine -- Zhenya.

-Once again, glad to meet you. Thank you… thank you very much for your help.

-No problem. I would like to leave you right in front of your place, but looking at the map it seems to me that it would take more than two hours.

-Yes, of course, there is no need. I live on the other side of Moscow, almost in the suburbs.

-I am building myself a villa not far from there. But unfortunately I will not go there today. I will leave you at "Polyanka", in the center. I live there. That's the gray line. You travel to the end and then catch the blue one, to Gorchakova Street. Is that right?

-Yes, of course. Once again, thank you.

-You're welcome. It's nice talking to you.

Natasha stared at Zhenya's face. She had nothing to fear. He looked good-natured, cheerful. He wore glasses, and when he smiled, dimples appeared on his cheeks.

-How old are you? -Natasha asked.

-I'm 25.

Natasha was surprised. So young, and already driving a nice car, living in the center of town and building his own villa. She asked him what he did for a living. He said he was a lawyer by education, and was doing something related to security in the subway. Natasha never understood exactly what.

-But my hobby is reading books.-he continued. -You know, sometimes I find books that people just leave on the street. I don't care if they're dirty or crushed. I still take them and examine them. Sometimes I find wonderful pieces of work.

-I do the same! Sometimes I wonder how people throw away so many amazing books just like that!

-I wonder the same thing.

- Right! Who is your favorite author?

-I don't have a favorite author. But I can tell you who I hate - Dostoevsky.

-How is it possible to hate Dostoevsky?

-When you read Dostoevsky, you feel like you're in hell. You fall into a bottomless pit and you can't get out.

-But you have to agree that he is a genius.

-Yeah, that's for sure.

The car was moving slowly in the rain. They were passing the Kremlin. Natasha began to hope that the traffic would continue a little longer. That it would take forever to reach the subway. It would soak, mold, rot from the rain. And that by the time they would get out of the car, a hundred years would have passed, and the world would still be just as wet and rustling.

She texted Dima not to go to the park, because she was on her way back anyway and to wait at home, on Gorchakova Street. He said that he'd guessed so and he already had gone home.

Evgeni kept laughing and talking about literature, theater, music, everything that made life meaningful.

It suddenly seemed to Natasha, quite unexpectedly, that the premature night would never cease to envelop the suns of the smooth domes, that the Kremlin would never shine, that all the streets, with the lights on them blurring into a huge diamond, were all uniting to form a new Moscow, unheard of, unseen by anyone.

-We arrived at Polyanka. -Zhenya announced.

Natasha began to put on her wet sneakers. Suddenly Zhenya thought of something and ran to the trunk.

-Do you drink wine?-he asked.

-Yes.

-White or red?

-Red.

-Take it.-he handed a bottle. -Have a drink tonight with your boyfriend.

-Oh, really… You don't have to!

-Take it! This is the last bottle of red wine in the car. Such wine is not sold in stores. It's imported by special order from Spain. It's impossible to get it.

-And how did you get it?

-A secret.-the dimples on his face flashed.

On the way to the subway, Natasha could not stop smiling. She smiled after that, in the subway, too and an hour later when she got out, she was still smiling. She looked drunk, and she hadn't taken a sip of the secret wine yet.

Suddenly, her life in Moscow seemed boring with Dima, the subway station and the long journey every day more disgusting than ever, his perpetual lateness awkward, his ordinary work, more wretched than ever. She imagined a life far more glamorous. Bolshoi theater, an evening dress and high heels… She had always dreamed of being taken there. And Dima, as it turned out later, had no such intentions.

Masha, his niece, opened the door.

-How are you, little one? - Natasha asked with some childish spirit. Dima was lying on the bed. They wanted to watch a movie, but they never agreed on which one, so in the end they didn't watch anything.

-Do you want red wine?-Natasha asked.

- Did you buy wine?

-Yes.

-How much did it cost?

-I don't remember anymore… 500 rubles.

-Oh, cheap. What is it?

-I don't know, I don't remember.

-Give me the bottle. Pff, semi-sweet. And I like dry wine. I don't feel like drinking.

Natasha sat on the bed and drank semi-sweet wine by herself. The next day he told her that they would not be able to go to St. Petersburg for the weekend because he did not have enough money. Natasha was upset. She had been waiting for this weekend the whole month. She had bought special underwear "for Petersburg" when they would be alone, in the hotel room, and no one would disturb them. But the underwear would remain unworn, the wine would remain unfinished.

Over the weekend, Dima announced that he had to work. And Zhenya- that he was free. So Natasha found herself at Polyanka metro station again. They took a walk. He asked her about her boyfriend. She told him that it was not serious, that he did not promise her anything about the future. That was true. "Let's wait and see" – he liked to say.

-If you want, you can move in with me, Natasha. Break up with him.

-Not yet. I'm not ready to break up with him.

-Then what are we going to do?

-We will wait.

Natasha started bringing a bottle of red semi-sweet wine home every week.

-You understand that what I'm doing is disgusting to me. I'm not that kind of a girl, it's not inherent in me, I can't recognize myself.

-Natasha, it's easy! Who do you like more - him or me?

-I feel like a girl with him. And with you-like a woman. Don't you understand, I don't want to be just one or the other!

She started coming home with new clothes. Dima didn't notice anything. He worked harder and harder and earned less and less. They made less and less love. And the truth is, she longed for him to notice the change, she longed for him to make a fuss and demand she stay, to never let go of her. But he kept on saying, "Let's wait and see."

One night Natasha announced that she would sleep at her mother's. An hour later she found herself in front of the Bolshoi Theater. She crossed the entrance with her new high heels. Her beautiful body was accentuated by a long black dress. And she had a charming gentleman with glasses holding her by the hand, a gentleman working on something to do with subway security, no one knew exactly what. They sat in the most expensive box, drank the most expensive champagne and they were happy - at least that's what it looked on the outside.

The next day she returned to Gorchakova Street. Masha opened the door for her. Natasha said "How are you, little one?" just like a woman.

She entered Dima's room. He was lying down on the bed.

-Hug me.

There was no sign of her body left. Only his hands were there in its place, strong, warm, tanned from the long work under the sun. So different from Zhenya's hands.

-My beauty.-Dima flattered her-With every single day you become more and more beautiful.

"If you don't hold on to me, I'll disappear."- Natasha thought.

-I missed you.

-I missed me, too.

He didn't understand, but he laughed.

Natasha stared eagerly at that smile, as if it were the last smile on earth.

-Stay here, hug me.

They snuggled together for a long time, each grieving for their own thing. It seemed to Natasha, quite unexpectedly, that it was raining again all over Moscow, that the streets were soaking wet once again, that hail was sweeping away all the gray leaves from the trees. There, far from the Kremlin, a new Moscow was being formed, unheard of, unseen by anyone. But there were no blurred diamonds of glass in it. There was only one beautiful, big chasm, and no one knew whether to jump into or not. No one knew, and nothing was known except that there were a few drops of semi-sweet wine left in the bottle.

Months without Julia

I woke up around seven in the morning. Generally, I don't wake up so early, but this morning there was a reason. Cigarette smoke from Julia's mouth. It went straight into my nostrils and tickled every molecule of my sleep with its nasty taste of death.

I looked at her. She was still naked. Her face was ugly, like that of any prematurely awakened grown-up woman. Julia was turning beautiful only after 11 am. Now her blond hair, dried from constant dyeing, fell tousled to her nipples, shadows under her eyes made her skin look even paler and she smoked. She smoked most unceremoniously like a prostitute who had once seduced men in her role of a smoker, but had forgotten that she was no longer beautiful, now only irritating with her obsessive habit. She looked like a caricature. I loved her just like that-ugly. I loved her both after 11 and as a caricature.

-Damn it, Julia, how many times have I told you not to smoke in bed!-I cried sleepily.

Generally, I am not an aggressive man. But sometimes this woman drives me crazy, especially if I've repeated something to her so many times. I immediately repented. I felt guilty that I spoke so loudly. But Julia didn't react. Only then did I notice that her eyes weren't moving. Only her lips moved, eagerly absorbing the cigarette smoke like a baby swallowing milk. Her eyes were fixed on the white smoky wall.

-Julia!- I said and pushed her by the shoulder.

She shook lightly, but did not react.

-What's the matter with you, Julia?

Her focused eyes looked at me stealthily. It was as if a fish was looking at me underwater. It didn't drive me crazy that she didn't speak, but that she didn't even try. She puffed the smoke one last time and flicked the butt away in the nightstand ashtray. Then she left the room.

I found her in the kitchen breaking eggs into the hot pan.

-Julia!

She hit the next egg on the edge of the pan and the bubbling fat splashed her. Julia screamed in pain, but continued feverishly tossing eggs as if it were a matter of life and death.

She had fried all the eggs together. A whole pile stood ready on the plate and she was now transferring the last three.

-Damn it, Julia, leave those eggs!-This time I shouted

really angrily, and squeezed her wrist.

She dropped the spatula and they fell to the ground. At that moment, Julia roared loudly, just like a small child.

We had breakfast in silence. She was already wearing clothes and had washed her face. 11 was approaching.

Julia put the fried eggs in her mouth somehow by force. She ate the first one, without the last bite, and then swallowed a whole cup of coffee. She went to the sink and vomited.

It was Sunday. We went for a walk every Sunday. I told her that if she didn't want to, we might not go out today, but she insisted.

I waited for her at the door as she was getting ready in the bathroom. She came out pretty and fresh, like a new woman. She had fixed her hair and put on make-up. She was wearing a beautiful summer dress. Only the shadows under her eyes remained.

As we walked in the park, I held her hand, but she didn't seem to be with me. Her fish-like eyes stared at me, and this time they tried to talk, but they couldn't. It wasn't until we sat by the lake that she said:

-Do you remember how when we met I asked you if you could love me even when the sun goes down? You laughed and asked: "When will the sun go down?", and I replied: "I don't know. Maybe after a long time, and maybe very soon."

-Yes, I remember.

-Well, the sun has gone down.

-I don't understand, Julia. It's only noon.

Julia looked at me with eyes drenched in disenchantment. It was as if I had looked at my own self and my blood froze. This is how she looked at me.

-That's what I expected. You will never understand. My sunsets are different. They come and go when they want. Sometimes they are all year round. When I met you, the sun had just risen. But less than two months have passed and it is already beginning to disappear. Lord, how short is happiness! Until recently, I woke up to a carnival and thought it would last forever, and today the streets are full of shit.

-But Julia, we can handle this together. I'll get you out of this sunset!

She looked at me devilishly indifferent and turned her head away.

-It's late. It's already dark.

-I still love you.

-I don't.

-Why are you punishing me like that?

-I punish you because you love me.

-Can't my love make the sun rise?

-Nothing can make the sun rise.

-Then I will be by your side and wait until it rises.

-Don't wait for it. It can take a long time.

-Then I will wait a long time.

-I'll kill you.

-I don't believe you.

A few days passed. Julia continued to fry eggs and vomit them. Most of the time she just cried. But scariest were the moments when she did nothing. She just lay on the bed with her eyes fixed on the smoky wall and looked dead. Even the black circles under her eyes were gone. Now her whole face was empty of color.

We no longer made love. She fell asleep on one side of the bed, I on the other. When I tried to cuddle her, she threatened to kill me.

-It's not intentional. You're just suffocating me, and if someone tries to suffocate me, I'll kill him in self-defense.

-I don't understand why you have to defend yourself from me.

-I'm not defending myself from you. I'm defending myself from suffocation. If you touch me, I will suffocate. I swear it drives me crazy when you touch me.

I offered to take her to a psychologist. She reacted very violently and did not want to listen to me. Then I brought a psychologist to our home. She was lying on the bed, staring at the damn wall again. The man introduced himself in two words and started asking her questions. I was standing in the corner of the room, blushing with shame. I told her:

-Julia, please, get out of bed.

-I'm not lying on the bed. I'm lying on the ground.

-You're lying on the bed.

-I'm lying on the ground. You have no idea how much I'm lying on the ground.

The psychologist was feverishly scribbling while listening to our little scandal, and that made me terribly nervous. He began to ask her how long she had been reluctant to eat and other such nonsense. When it came to the topic of the pills she needed, Julia grabbed the ashtray from the nightstand and threw it at the doctor. It didn't hit. The ashtray was plastic and it rattled hollowly against the wall like a worn-out battle, like laughter loaded with vitiation.

Julia shrank into a ball of shame. For the first time since sunset, her face took on a color similar to red, and she seemed to be choking with self-remorse. But just when it looked as if she were about to burst in all directions, like a planet nearing its end, she mustered up some courage and got into the ring again.

-Go to hell, you and your fucking pills!

The psychologist pulled me aside and led me out into the hallway.

-The problem is quite clear. Manic depression. It can be serious. Go to the pharmacy today. I wrote you a prescription.

How long has she been lying on the bed like that?

Something about this doctor made me extremely nervous. I wished I had a glass ashtray in me.

I shouted at him as loud as my voice could shout: -Didn't you understand that this is not a bed? Didn't you understand that, you idiot?

Then I started weeping like a real idiot. My face turned into a ball of ice cream that kept melting.

I sent the doctor to the door. He said nothing more. Then I went back to Julia and lay down next to her on the ground. We cried all afternoon. She from depression, I from love.

The next day I left her. I didn't have the strength to live like that every day. She understood me. She just said:

-Better.

Then she looked at me again with her fish eyes, infused with some new form of madness and wisdom. It was as if I saw myself from outside again. This time I looked without my blood freezing. I understood that it was better.

A few days passed without Julia. Then months without Julia. A lifetime passed by, but the sky remained just as gloomy as the day she said "better".

One day I saw her on the street. She was more beautiful than ever. The sun had risen again. She smiled at me. My heart softened with pure hatred.

-I don't understand just one thing.- I told her. -Why did I love you so much and you never loved me, not even for a second, my dear?

Julia smiled at me again with some feminine, almost inaccessible grief and said, without looking at me at all:

-I loved you. If I didn't love you, I would never have kicked you out.

Sabina's High Heel

Sabina put on thick lipstick. Then she ran her fingers through her hair to ruffle it. She was known among men as "the wild cat." She had to maintain that image. Last touches and she was ready to go on stage. Perfume - that rich musk that brought to mind a woman's juices. Her satin corset, red, although soon she would be left with garters only.

The men looked at her in amazement. Out of all the strippers in this club, she was the most experienced. It was even rumored that the manager would soon cede part of the shares to her, because in addition to being very beautiful, she had the sharp mind of an entrepreneur. Nonetheless, Sabina had no ambitions to appear as a business lady. Unlike most erotic dancers, who worked as such only until they got on their feet and then hurried to erase their embarrassing pasts, it gave her real pleasure to be watched. It was the ecstasy that flowed through her body as dozens of men took a very small sip of whiskey, sticking in their throats like dry excitement, which made Sabina dance so vehemently. It was more than mania for attention. It was passion, it was the sadistic pleasure that out of all the men who want her madly, no one will really have her.

It was no secret that Sabina did not act like the other strippers. The naive girls, called from the tables by waving green papers in hand, were an object of her ridicule. They could receive five, sometimes even ten men in their little boudoirs a night. Sabina accepted only one, and only the one she liked.

She didn't wait for a man to make her an offer. If that happened, the poor creature would be looked at mockingly by those who already knew. Some had been coming to the club for years, with only the secret hope that Sabina would look at them. No success. No one had ever been able to figure out the unknown ways in which she chose a lover for the night. It wasn't the richest. It wasn't the most handsome, it wasn't the ugliest. It wasn't the fattest or the skinniest, it wasn't the intellectual, it wasn't the fool, it wasn't even the gentleman who wanted her the most. Sometimes it was the exact opposite- she chose that man in the crowd who looked at her with contempt. But even the strategy of treating Sabina with disdain or indifference didn't work. The next time she chose someone who brought her flowers and candies.

Sabina finished her last dance for the evening. Everyone, even the waiters in front of the small smoky stage, froze for a moment. This was the moment everyone was looking forward to. For some, even the subject of evening bets. Will it be that shy boy in the corner holding a cigarette in his thin transparent fingers, coughing out the smoke? He must be here for the first time, and he doesn't even pretend to like the show. Poor creature. Sabina likes them stupid, so that she can play with them as she pleases. Will it be that old tycoon in the leather booth, surrounded by all the other strippers? He, it seems, is already drooling over her and doesn't even glance at any of those beauties who, drunk and greedy, would do anything to distract him. Well, what about that man in the middle of the room, medium tall, medium handsome, with glasses and, apparently, from the middle class, ordering a medium-expensive champagne that he drinks in medium-sized sips? He must be a father of one or two children, have a wife and an acceptable apartment somewhere in the suburbs of Amsterdam. If only he knew how lucky is he about to become! His whole life will turn upside down in a second, just after Sabina's gaze.

But no. It's not him either. Sabina looks at them all, like a spoiled predator glancing at a herd of newborn sheep. She doesn't look for too long. Only superficially. However, any man who is shot by her ruthlessly indifferent eyes feels it: that whiskey in the throat is beginning to boil.

There he is. That's him. Some short man, about thirty, thirty-five. Black-eyed, with bulging veins and teeth that glow in a blurred smile. She gazes at him. No need to ask "Is it me?" It's him. When Sabina's eyes freeze, everyone knows the game is over.

The man gets up and goes to the prostitute. They sink behind the scenes. From that moment on, no one knows what is happening. Even those who have already been with her never talk about it. Some cheap music starts playing in the club. Some kind of lively, merry, vulgar pop, to dull the bad mood of all the others - the unelected. Those unworthy of Sabina. Of a cheap whore, as they put it. They wave to the waiter, order another whiskey. They drink it all at once, laugh and talk about their sexual achievements. All of them, meticulously hiding that their heart is a little broken. The tycoon chooses two of the strippers. They giggle flatteringly and, holding his hand, lead his flushing face to the boudoirs. He, like all the other men, is furious.

Mr.Black-Eyed finds himself in a dark room. His heart beats madly with rare excitement. Not arousal, but fear of the unexpected. This woman brings him the adrenaline that every man longs for.

-Lie down.-Sabina tells him.

The man goes to the bed.

-Not on the bed.

The man moves obediently to the ground.

-What's your name?

-Brian.

-Brian.- Sabina repeats.

The way she says it makes the man shudder. What an honor that this heartless woman, this monster, remembers his name. Unwillingly, he finds himself ready to do anything for her.

-Lie down on your stomach, Brian.

Brian does it.

-Now, Brian, hold your hands on your back.

Brian does it.

-Now, Brian…

Brian does everything Sabina tells him. But some things he doesn't do right. Then Sabina punishes him.

At first, Brian likes it. They do the same with small children. When they are obedient, they receive a small reward, when they are bad- a small punishment. Brian feels just like a child, Sabina just like a teacher. For all these years of experience she has learned only one thing - that you should treat men like little boys.

Then Brian starts to hurt. He begins to moan, groan and scream. He wants to escape from here, from this evil witch who mocks the very core of his existence. She humiliates everything in him - his body, his spirit, if there is one left, humiliates even the way this person feels pain. She continues to crush, to break, to shatter every fiber of his self-esteem, until in the end he is left with nothing, a moaning soul on which some prostitute mercilessly steps.

Any other torturer at this point would shut the mouth of his victim. Everyone, but Sabina. She has another method, much more effective, for destroying the man.

-Brian.- she tells him- If you keep screaming, it will hurt a lot more.

Brian falls silent. Tears flow from his eyes. He can't breathe. He chokes on his own snot and his saliva spilled around like a puddle.

Sabina continues with the torture. Brian strives to be as quiet as possible. But from time to time, he happens to make a small sound. This sound is inevitable. It is the wheezing of the lungs when the swallowed saliva begins to flow to their bottom. It is, if you will, the delayed cough, when a new dose of dust from the dirty floor hits his throat. Brian strains his whole consciousness to the last of his strength not to make a sound, but at one point his body surrenders. He jumps from the edge and begins to fight for his life, for that breath of air that may be his last.

Then, as Sabina has warned, it hurts a lot more. This pain is unthinkable. It is not from her whip, which until then had played everywhere on his blue skin. It is not the blades of those steel spikes, nor is it that iron rod that is hot.

This is Sabina's high heel. It cuts into his ribs like thunder, tears every purple cloud in the night sky and makes him bleed. It makes Brian think that if he wants something more than anything else in this world, or in this case, his only wish, it is, as ridiculous as it may sound, that the clouds were not made of cotton.

At one point, Brian stops thinking at all. His nervous system refuses to function. No matter how much it hurts, no matter how much he suffers, he can't take it anymore. He jumps from the edge for the last time without thinking about the consequences, and indulges in a squeaky, long, pitiful cry. Sabina keeps kicking him with her heel. This time it doesn't work. No matter how much she kicks, Brian keeps writhing.

This makes Sabina angry. For the first time, she is out of control. She begins to think how much more she can hurt him, what trick to invent with her heel. And in this helplessness to create something different, he keeps kicking harder and harder.

At one point, Brian's crying subsides. The attention to his own pain is replaced by surprise. Suddenly he realizes that Sabina has stopped kicking. He finds a broken high heel in front of his eyes.

Brian looks at the heel. A heel like any other. For any man, this would be the end of the night adventure with the most mysterious prostitute in Amsterdam. For anyone, but for Brian. Because as he feels the untying of his arms and legs, as he listens to the sound of garters rising and the lighting of a cigarette, as the last streams of blood dry on his skin, Brian stares at this silly, green, eight-inch high heel and remembers.

He remembers everything. Their first night together. When he encouraged her to hurt him. They were both so miserable. He suffered from self-hatred. She suffered from the same. But they were very different. She wanted to infect with self-hatred all that surrounded her, he-to be infected even more by hers. A wild form of gangrene, which, in the mind of the leper, would be sweetest when it fully manages to take over.

He remembers their first holding of hands. Then he had managed to sneak from the boys' floor to the girls' floor with the help of some animal force that had allowed him to jump over his ledge and climb up the half-rotten tree. She awaited him sitting on her bed with her braids untied and a cheap perfume she had managed to steal from some classmate, even though he had told her he wasn't sure he was coming because they could catch him, or he might fall off the tree. However, both of them secretly knew, with that infallible intuition of the first love, that this encounter would take place. The window was deliberately opened. He gripped her ledge with his burning fingers. She saw him and laughed loudly. She didn't help him get in. Even then she looked at him with a contemptuous satisfaction. She liked the way he struggled to reach her. Finally, panting and sweating, Brian took a final breath and pushed his way up to the cherished goal.

He sat on her bed and looked at her. She was cross-legged like the grown-up ladies and wore vulgar high heels she had mugged from God knows where. Her dress was short and crumpled. The only dress she had. Beneath the neckline, though disguised, was an indelible stain. Still, she was unimaginably beautiful, and Brian couldn't stop staring at her as if she were a goddess.

The next day he came again. The first kiss. She said to him:

-Brian, I'm not that easy.

-Then I'll come again tomorrow.

It was a miracle that none of the guards caught them. The boys and girls in this orphanage slept apart, because we all know what happens otherwise…

But she was cunning. When she got pregnant, even Brian didn't understand. She was just fifteen, and she could already hurt herself so badly. However, Brian sensed something was wrong and whispered:

-If you want, we can just hold hands tonight.

Then she cried for a very long time.

It was the closest thing to "I love you" that she would ever hear.

Brian looked at Sofia. That was her real name.

- Sofia, don't you remember me?

-I'm not sure,-she murmurs, annoyed. She hates people from the past to show up.

-Don't you remember anything about the two of us?

-No.

She turns the lights up. Her make-up, though expensive, is beginning to smear and she now looks so mundane, so, if you will, pitifully ugly. A cheap bed with white duvets shines in the corner. The whole room looks so pitifully grim.

For the first time, she looks carefully at his face. Then she realizes she's finally found the man she's been looking for all these years. She loses control. She collapses at his feet. She finds herself lying there indefinitely, trembling as if swaying on the waves of some stormy sea, clutching the man's legs like a life raft. She doesn't moan, but Brian is already smiling. If he wants to take revenge, now is the best moment.

He watches her with contemptuous pleasure as her helpless body writhes in his shadow. He points his rough hand at her, his hand heavy with pain and rage. But suddenly something in that hand softens and he unwillingly finds himself weak, struck by tenderness.

He says:

-Come on, give me your hand.

She holds out her hand to him, and he helps her get to

her feet.

But she is weak, very weak, and she slips into his arms.

He leads her to the bed and they lie there completely silent, as in the good old days.

For the first time since becoming a prostitute, Sabina has somebody spend the night in her bed.

The Winter and Summer of a Helium Balloon

There are different types of rivers. Some are small, others big. Some are beautiful, others nothing special. But all of them have something in common – they bring back memories.

Here is the Vltava. Do you remember how we walked along it one winter night? Of course you do. You were in your black coat, I in my big blue jacket. I dreamed of summer, when the extra clothes would be useless, when everything would be lighter and nicer. Then, maybe just then, I would actually be happy.

I took you by the arm so that I don't lose you. You were so far away. When I was a child, they used to buy me helium balloons. Who would have guessed that this would teach me how to deal with you? But you don't know something else. I took you by the arm so that you don't end up losing me.

We hardly talked anymore. You lit cigarette after cigarette. And we said ~ bye ~, and you kissed me on the lips, and I didn't feel anything towards you.

When two people are helium balloons, the question is which one will take off first. The answer was me. But you know I didn't do it on purpose. You just forgot to hold me.

Here it is, the Vltava again, but in the summer. Everything is lighter and nicer. Now I know that there are things that weigh more than a winter jacket. They are not visible. And then --not now --just then I might have actually been happy.

Not all people are helium balloons. Some are ordinary balloons. I can't stand that some people forget how to fly. That's why I'm afraid for you. You, for me -- not anymore. We sit by the river and the sun shines in our eyes. You close yours, so that you don't go blind, and I close mine for another reason. You wouldn't see this anyway. But if my eyes were canvases and the sun was an artist, it would dip its brush in a lake, all alone, and it would reflect itself half-way. That's when I know my soul is painted with watercolors.

We talk a lot. And we say ~ bye ~. And you don't kiss me on the lips.

If you want to make a helium balloon fall, you have to pierce it with a needle. But who would have guessed that some balloons fall due to *lack* of piercing? Now, if you wish, you can keep me forever. But you let the wind blow me away.

Since then, I've crossed many rivers. Much bigger, but all empty.

The Last Word on Earth

It was December 31st. For most people, this is known as New Year's Eve. For me, it was just the 473rd day of my life without sex.

I had an arrangement with some strangers to watch the fireworks on Trafalgar Square. You will ask why strangers? Because I never have friends in London.

So we got together in a pub in Soho. We chose it on a simple principle - it was the only one around that didn't have an entrance fee. There was a reason for that, of course - it closed at 10:30 pm, there was mostly cheap low-quality beer and there was nowhere to sit. In general, the perfect choice.

At first we all felt a little awkward. As you can guess, we were all foreigners in this group. And while we tried to deceive ourselves and the others that the only reason we were there was because we wanted to meet new people and expand our boundaries, the truth was the same for all of us — there was simply no one else to celebrate with on this day.

The group was diverse. There was a Mongolian guy with questionable demeanor, a shy Iraqi girl with a quiet voice , a very emotional Malaysian girl, a Turk posing as a Brit, a Brit of Indian origin and an Irishman who was trying to hit on me. Since I took account of this fact, I took the effort to remember his name - the only name I remembered - Aaron.

Aaron approached me, seeing that I was tactfully but tirelessly trying to get rid of the strange Mongolian, "stole" me for a minute, friendly-wrapped his arm around my waist, and asked me where I was from. He went speechless the moment I told him I was Bulgarian. I began to wonder if he and the Malaysian girl had accidentally exchanged skins in the bathroom. He was so excited that tears almost welled up in his eyes.

-Bulgaria! Oh, Bulgaria! My previous girlfriend was Bulgarian!

With that confession, I said to myself "aha." The business became clear. He is one of those guys who always fondly remember their exes, even when they are already married and have three kids. No, that was not a good sign. He was not at all embarrassed by the fact that he began courting a new woman with tearful memories of the previous one, but continued:

-Oh, Bulgaria! I love your food! There is no such food anywhere else! And my girlfriend… and my ex-girlfriend, she was from Plovdiv! From which city are you from?

-I am from Plovdiv, too.

-Oh, really? Oh, Plovdiv! I love this city. She, my girlfriend… my ex, I mean, her name was Elena. Now I will show her to you on Facebook. Maybe you know her?

-No, I don't know her.

At that moment, for some reason, the conversation abruptly ended. We both stared at the bar in awkward silence. Aaron got so embarrassed that he removed his hand from my waist. Then, so as not to shed another tear, he decided to change the subject and asked me if I wanted anything from the bar. A good sign at last, I thought.

I chose gin and tonic. He had a beer. For him that was one beer more, and for me the first gin and tonic after two beers. This cheered me up a little, and I finally started laughing like the Malaysian, acting weird like the Mongolian, and flirting like the drunken Irishman. In all this turmoil, the Iraqi girl said one quiet: "Goodbye, I'm leaving." and waved uncertainly at the door. The next moment she evaporated like a ghost and we never saw her again. Poor girl, what will she do on New Year's Eve all by herself? She couldn't even get drunk.

I soon noticed that a new person had showed up -- a black guy from New York. His presence for some reason cheered me up even more. I approached him and started blabbering on about the sights in and around London to show how smart I was. He questioned me for a long time about the palace in Windsor, until it finally turned out that he himself had been there. Then we had some good laughs and the more I looked at his perfect, large teeth, which he boldly revealed with each new burst of laughter, the funnier things became. I had completely forgotten about my Irishman when he approached again, grabbed me by the waist and "stole me for a minute." Alas, he didn't buy me any more alcohol. And the bar was starting to close. I finished my last beer fast. Money for entrance fees was, of course, not to be wasted by any of us, so we had to spend the rest of the night outside, on the nasty, cold streets of London. Exactly at the last moment we were joined by some Greek girl and boy who were friends. And the group was ready to embark on their little New Year's adventure.

We decided to go to Chinatown. Most restaurants there were open because the Chinese were the only ones who didn't give a fuck about New Year's Eve. We chose a fast food diner that looked pretty decent. The Malaysian and the Mongolian went inside. But when the rest of us headed to the front door, guards stood in front of us and prevented us from entering.

-What the hell is wrong?

-We do not accept more people.

We stayed stranded at the door like stray dogs. The

Malaysian asked the guards to let us in.

-We are together! Please, please!

-Just one more!

The New Yorker didn't wait for a second chance, and before we could blink, he was on the other side of the glass door.

-Damn it! It's harder to enter this stupid diner than a nightclub with a dress code! - I nagged.

-Well, if they dumped us, we'll dump them, too. - Aaron said.

I don't know if that was a reference to a previous event in his life or an attempt to eliminate as much of his competition as possible, but all of us were damn hungry, so the Greeks, Aaron and I decided to look for another place.

-Of course, later we'll meet again. - I said- Later, when we're done with dinner.

-Yes, later, later. -Aaron replied.

We walked down the busy street, intoxicated by the general New Year's ecstasy, the orange lanterns above our heads, the colorful windows of Chinese restaurants, and we no longer thought of anything heavy. It was as if we had become as light as the lanterns themselves, as if the gin itself had turned us into spirits, as if nothing could break us down anymore. Nothing but the memories -- and they were somewhere far away. We forgot we were alone, because at that moment, briefly, we were not; we forgot that we were cold, because at that moment, briefly, we were not; we forgot that each of us, recently or long ago, once or many times, has been dumped because at that moment (briefly) we were not. "Fuck the old year!" - we all thought. "There's only an hour left of it. And after that one hour, everything will be behind us! All the shit will be behind us! And all the good things will come true!"

No one wanted that more than I did.

Aaron and the Greek found some small stinky place with ungodly prices. Oh, these Chinese bastards, how cunning they'd become! £6.50 for a box for home and 11.50 if you want to eat inside. The other girl and I decided not to eat. We weren't so hungry anyway. While we waited for the boys, we stayed inside by the door so that we don't freeze outside. A Chinese woman insisted that we eat. We said we were just waiting for our friends to get some food. And again they kicked us out like stray dogs.

- What nonsense! - I continued to protest- We can't even enter a dirty Chinese restaurant!

Soon the boys came out with a box of Chinese crap. I took nothing but a spring roll from Aaron. Then I chewed the spare dessert from my pocket. Good that I foresaw what kind of nonsense London would be on New Year's Eve.

Full or almost full, we were ready to welcome the new decade. We lined up on Trafalgar Square like the thousands of other dumbasses waiting for the New Year's fireworks.

In the mutual chat we were trying to meet the others. But this, of course, was the most sarcastic joke in the history of New Year's holidays. Drunken teens, mothers with children, and Asians with cameras were shouting from all directions. I started taking bets with myself on which one I would get first -- claustrophobia or a panic attack. And yet, just when it couldn't get any worse, I don't know where or how the British Turk sprung up. Either he had followed us all the time without our noticing, or he was once a hodja with clairvoyant abilities. He clung to me, and no one, not even the Irishman under the influence of alcohol, could get me out at this point. After a few cheap jokes that I tried to laugh at, and endless attempts to send Aaron telepathic signals for help, I finally managed to get back to him, just before the first fireworks pierced the ass of the old year and flooded the sky with bloody diarrhea. This event made everyone scream with excitement, including me, and even more excitedly to open bottles of champagne. Or in our case, coke with rum in a plastic bottle.

Then came a few more disappointing fireworks, which were no different from the previous ones and it was time for the long journey home. We couldn't meet the others. I didn't give sex to the black guy and rightly so - he stole my burger. I didn't kiss Aaron, and he didn't kiss me either, I didn't party with the Greeks, and I couldn't get in touch with the Malaysian girl. Only the Turk -- I don't know how -- appeared next to me in the middle of the long queue to the subway. I had to wait with him. Then, of course, we split up after he tried again to kiss me for the New Year.

Honestly, I was dying to get home. But when I got out of Turnham Green Station and saw that the windows of my little house were still shining, I decided to hit the streets for another hour. I didn't feel like going home at all now. Ronald, Brandon and my mother would have welcomed the New Year with mediocre conversations and expensive but bitter champagne, my mother would secretly cry about "our bad relationship", and I would have to take a long, boring shower with lukewarm water just to avoid others in the same room. Everything would be terribly depressing. Especially now, after the holiday was over and there was nothing more to expect.

I managed to get into a bar just long enough to take a piss before they closed. Then I went to another, but they were closing as well. They didn't even let me in. Just when hope had begun to fade, and I walked down the empty street with nostalgic memories of the previous New Year's, in 2019, when I had hit on a drunken Englishman from the same bar where I managed to take a piss, a boy on a bicycle stopped next to me. He didn't look like a drunken nuisance trying to hit on everyone he met, or a midnight maniac running away from a mental hospital. In fact, he looked relatively sober. He kindly asked me if I wanted a beer. So, satisfactorily adequate. I agreed. He took a bottle of beer out of his leather bag that said "Fuck Boris" and opened it for me. I drank.

-Aren't you going to drink?- I asked him.

- That was my last beer.

- Okay. And why did you give it to me?

- I don't know. Just like that.

That instantly won my trust and I invited him to look for an open bar together. He locked his bike to a street lamp and started walking with me. I took the opportunity to peer into his eyes. They were bluish-green.

-This is fucking Chiswick! Everything closes at 2 o'clock at night, even on New Year's Eve. This is the most snobbish neighborhood in the world!

-What is your name?

-Leopold. And yours?

-Nina.

-Nice to meet you, Nina.

-Where are you from?

-From Germany. And you?

-From Bulgaria.

I paused in anticipation. Nothing about an ex-girlfriend. I relaxed. We continued walking along the street. Everything was closing.

-Do you smoke weed?- he suddenly broke the silence.

-Weed...? Yes, but very rarely. - I replied

absentmindedly- Listen, there seems to be no point in looking for a place.

-Yes, I think you're right... Let's go to my house and get drunk like pigs!

-Umm... look, not that... I'm sure you're a good boy and so on, but I'm not used to going to the houses of strangers I've just met on the street.

("I lied a little" - I thought- "I meant I didn't do it anymore.")

The German laughed sincerely and then replied:

-Yes, yes, I understand. I didn't want it to sound like that. Well, okay, I'm going home anyway because I'm fucking freezing! It was nice to chat!

-Wait a minute... What were you just saying... about that weed?

He laughed again.

-I have some weed with me.

-I think I can stay with you for a joint. We'll smoke it quickly and go home.

-Well, okay.

I found a place -- some outside staircase in a residential yard. The house looked dead. All you had to do was jump over a small fence. I jumped it first. He followed me. He opened his bag and began to search.

-Oh, shit! I don't think I have any more.

I sighed in disappointment.

-Well…at least we found a place to sit.

-I have hashish. You want some?

-Hashish? Yes, even better.

He rolled up two cigarettes and handed one to me.

I was smoking and laughing at myself. Who would have guessed that I would welcome 2020 like this - with some anarchist German on a London staircase in an expensive snobbish neighborhood, smoking hashish practically under my mother's nose?

-What do you do alone on New Year's Eve? - I asked him.

-Well, my roommates are gone. They are all somewhere else. And my family is in Germany.

-Do you have a good family?

-Yes, my parents are quite cool. The last time they came to visit me, we smoked together. And how is yours?

-Oh… let's talk about something else.

-All right. I won't ask. And besides that, some things just can't be said with words.

-What do you mean?

-Isn't it crazy that words just aren't enough? Never, for nothing. Words are always smaller and less than what we want to express. And to explain the words, you need other words. All words are just derivatives of other words and all other words are meaningless too. How many dictionaries have been created and they're never enough for people to understand each other!

I remembered the dictionaries I found in a cafe in Oxford. They were set aside to complement the interior. But I decided to take a look at them. It turned out that for each letter there was a separate dictionary. I accidentally opened the pages of the letter "c", trying to find new words and memorize them. I never saw words as an obstacle. I saw them as a bridge. Each word was full of colors, lights and melodies. Some words were full of mornings, and some words were full of nights. Some words were full of love, but most were heartbreaking. How many nights have I stood over words, weeping over them! How many nights have I wandered through my grandfather's dictionaries, drenched in dust and laziness, trying to gather in words! Trying to arrange them, trying to hide them in my skirt like autumn apples, to keep them safe right to the doorstep of my home, to polish them! How many times have I tried to give them away to strangers just to put a smile on their face? And how many of these apples were thrown in the dust by ungrateful people who believed they were nonsense, a trivial gift that could be replaced in the store right away? How many of these apples were eaten by worms? How many of these apples were sour, hard, or too sweet? How many of these apples were as juicy as fragrant honey? Probably just one… And I lost it, too.

Where were all those dictionaries now that my grandfather has died? Who is guarding them now? Do you think that dictionaries will just stay in the same room forever!? They must be guarded constantly! They will fly away… That's why the books have covers, to turn themselves into birds, and when no one looks at them they just fly away. If they are lucky, they get caught and healed, if they are not, they get killed and eaten by other dictionaries, by other books. How many dictionaries have been destroyed forever?

And here I am, the last person on Earth trying to save a bird. With a man who doesn't like to talk. But let me tell you something, dear friend. Birds are not saved by verbosity. Birds are saved by a single crumb. Otherwise they gain weight and can no longer fly.

I myself don't like to talk. I love writing. And I tell him.

-I myself don't like to talk. I love writing.

-Maybe one day you'll write something about me. And I'll read it, too. You will become the next world-famous writer. I'm going to tell people that I met this… what was your name?

-Nina Zhelyazkova.

-Nina Zhe- ly-az-ko-va…

-And what was yours?

-Leopold. You can call me Leo.

-Leo. That's easy. So what, Leo? We froze our asses. I think it's time to go home.

-Yes… that's right. By the way, do you want more beer?

-You said you gave me the last one, didn't you?

- We can buy more.

-Where from?

-I know an Indian shop. It's 24/7.

-But on New Year's Eve?

-Indians and Chinese are the only ones who don't give a fuck about The New Year.

We sit on the street and chew some samosa while our noses keep dripping. Between snots, short conversations and chattering teeth, we sip some fictional beer. Our hands are red from holding the iced can. And I forget that I've forgotten that I was cold.

-Yeah… These Indians are the best.

-Are you cold?-Leo says. -I can give you my gloves.

He takes some gloves out of his pocket. He hands them to me. I put them on. We walk slowly down the street. We stop at the corner next to my house. The lights have already gone out. We finish our beer.

Leo unlocks his bike. Now his eyes do not look like blueish-green, but greenish-blue. What color are they actually?

We say goodbye. He leaves. But before he dissolves around the corner, he suddenly turns to me.

-What's wrong?

He pulls his bike next to me.

-I forgot something… I forgot to take my gloves.

-Okay.

I take off the gloves. I hand them back to him.

-You know what? I agree to go to your house and get drunk like pigs. Then we'll take a long and hot bath, you have a bath, don't you, then we'll have some long and extremely tender sex, because we are both insanely lonely, we'll fall in love with each other, we'll have the most amazing night of our lives, we will not talk at all and tomorrow, that is, today, at 10 o'clock in the morning, I'll leave you without any pretensions, I'll pack my bags with a disgusting hangover, I'll look at my crying mother with extremely upset nerves, who will repeat to me how much our relationship has deteriorated , how I never share anything with her and how we are so far apart that one day we'll stop talking at all, and I would know that this day has long come; I'll quickly make up some story for her, for example that after the fireworks I slept at a friend's in Soho, she doesn't really know that I have no friends, then I'll hug her without a drop of desire, because that way I'll only upset myself, I'll get in the car with Ronald and he'll take me to Heathrow Airport. And we'll miss each other madly, Leo, and we'll never see each other again or we'll see each other again, but it won't be the same and we'll just wait for this old, fucking 2020 to end so that we cease feeling, albeit briefly, so fucking lonely, freezing or dumped. And maybe next year we'll find true love. Or we never will. -I tell him in my head.

He must be telling me something similar.

Then we say goodbye for the last time.

White Christmas

The winter of 2020. I had gathered with some losers who had mistakenly stayed in Bulgaria during the events, which everyone soon called 'that thing', wandered through the streets of Sofia like homeless beggars and lived in blissful ignorance for the future, getting drunk every night like pigs. The only thing that distinguished me from them was that I spoke Bulgarian. Their names were, in alphabetical order, Fer, a former Lima musician who had taught me to dance salsa, Brad, a terribly sexy Englishman, the living incarnation of 21st-century Don Juan (with the sole exception that Don Juan was a rich and skilful seducer, and this one was just trying to fuck every breathing creature with a cunt that he met, relying on his one and only special trick – to get the poor thing wasted with a bottle of cheap gin mixed with plenty of tonic), Brad's cousin, who didn't look bad at all, but since he was accompanied by Don Juan, he was always in his natural shadow (I don't remember exactly what he was called), Stefano, an Italian with a Swiss approach to life -- politically neutral and indifferent to everyone (although this seemed to be due not to a moral system of principles, but some other substances that we will now avoid mentioning for the sake of keeping the story short), Blanca - a Spanish bitch who most of the time ground her ass onto someone, William - another Englishman, whose distinguishing characteristics, according to his roommates, were that he farted all night and loved to kiss the muscles of his arms, and about 10 other similar crackheads, which, so as not to bore the reader, I will not list.

We went to a bar. You will ask – what bar? -- after all everything was closed. Well…The truth was that some bars were operating illegally, and since they knew us well, they let us in as special guests. It was enough for Fer to put his charming smile into action, to say a few kind words to the hostess, who at that moment looked cautiously in all directions, and in less than a second, 20 people poured in like a shaken sack of potatoes. Then the heavy door closed, the lights went on again, and a really frantic party like the ones in the Great Gatsby was starting to take place inside. The only difference was that ours were a little more illegal.

It was surprisingly quiet tonight. Most people were at home, as befits a truly exemplary Christian country. After all, it happened to be December 24th. However, I knew that Christmas was a fabrication that came as a disguised version of the cult of the Sun God, whom people have worshiped since the dawn of humanity, that the Virgin Mary is just a Christianized image of the Bulgarian goddess Hecate, and a bunch of other goddesses from our sacred lands, so in short, the celebration of Christmas paradoxically makes you a true pagan. Which I don't mind, of course. I myself happen to be a bit of a pagan - and how do we know what people did before to worship the Sun-God? I bet they had midnight orgies in anticipation of the sunrise, drank liters of red wine and took drugs like chamomile, crocuses, exotic varieties of wild mushrooms and whatever else was present on the planet back then. And who are we to oppose ancient traditions?

So I lit a cigarette, sat on the couch and started talking to Fer about astrology, tarot cards, music, the reasons why Bulgaria and Peru are not known for their contribution to world culture and other such nonsense. He and I had become inseparable lately. We had exactly the same views on life, exactly the same blatant and adventurous nonchalance, the same call for freedom, the same dreams of strenuous and filthy crossings of the globe. He added that he did not believe in zodiac signs at all, but since we were both Aquarius, we obviously understood each other. Just don't start thinking that there was something… a bit more special between us. The last thing I wanted in my life was to start a love affair with another wanker. Fer was just a very dear friend to me, like a brother I had dreamed of for a long time. If we have to be honest -- in this separate and specific moment of the earth's timeline -- my only brother, my only friend.

Brad took the opportunity to jump into the other seat next to me and offered me a glass of gin and tonic. I took the tonic because, god, did I not want to drink that night, swallowed the blissful liquid like a shot, and dumped him, going to play pool with the others. While I was waiting for my turn, I met some weird Russian guy who studied medicine in Bulgaria. He puffed cigarette after cigarette, drank like an animal, and in a very strange way reminded me terribly of the last boy I had desperately fallen in love with. I looked at the Russian one more time, saw that he was exactly the same piece of shit as the previous one, and concluded, "I like him." I asked him why he smoked and drank so much if he was going to become a doctor, and he replied that smoking and drinking was the only way to survive along the way to a medical degree. "A satisfactory answer. - I thought - I like him. "

My turn came. The Russian said he was going somewhere and would definitely be back in five minutes to continue our conversation. I drank from Fer's beer. I concentrated. Of course, I didn't hit the pocket. We were joined by a Frenchman who taught me to say 'win' in French - I don't know why, since we weren't winning anything. William grumbled about his blow and touched his lips softly onto his muscles. A ball of smoke swirled around the table. The Russian never came back, Fer and I were ravaging beer after beer, and some Israeli girl was crying in the corner. According to the Frenchman her name was Josephine. I asked Josephine why she was crying and she started telling me about some Englishman who had broken her heart a few days ago and whom she had met by chance at this bar. The two of us started swearing at him – she -- a little more inse-curely, I – like a real truck driver, ready to kill for my new sister. Then she treated me to a shot of whiskey, which was okay by me. I decided to continue to support her in her emancipation as an independent woman, especially if that would help me mooch more to drink. And after all, I didn't mind learning how Brad was in bed - as expected, a complete parody.

On the couch in the other room, where I had last left him, we saw our prince on a lame horse again. He was sitting next to Blanca and stroking her thighs. She was reclining on the couch like the pure Mother Mary herself during the Immaculate Conception, drinking her beer as if she was not noticing any of the sacrileges being performed on the temple of her body. The cousin stared into space with a dull, slightly upset look. The Russian lit his next cigarette and spoke with some arousing nostalgia, archetypal version of a 2005 *chalga* singer with naturally bleached hair. We returned to the room with the pool table. My team was really winning. How long had Josephine and I been missing from the game, then?

Fer scored the final ball and we started jumping around in ecstasy. The Frenchman kissed me on the cheek. I started repeating " *J'ai gagné*" because I didn't know what the conjugation of the verb in first person plural was. Then some more people joined, as might be expected, Fer's friends, and shots and mugs began pouring in like summer rain (in the other room, only god knows what else). No one knew exactly how much time we spent drinking, but one thing was for sure - about seconds before Christmas, everyone had fallen under the tables like bruised pears. And as it happens in some magical moments on holidays, events had changed course and now everything was going backwards.

Blanca was making out with Brad's cousin. Brad stood alone in the empty corner, talking to himself. I passed by and heard that he was very lonely, that his whole childhood was a mess and that he had a terrible relationship with his mother. "It reminds me of me." I said to myself. I sat on the other end of the couch and started crying with him. Half an hour later, I tried to wipe away my tears. Then I realized I had never cried - at least not on the outside. Eyewitnesses say that we had just sat there and laughed, each to himself, without saying a word to the other. Then, slightly dizzy, we had gotten up, shaken hands, and patted each other on the backs like old mates.

We finally found Stefano - he was sitting alone in the toilet trying to find someone to borrow a credit card from. Brad's face got back to his joker mask and began to make his stupid jokes. "So we're finally gonna get our white Christmas," he giggled. "Well, let it snow!" William and Stefano laughed too, and then they all turned their backs to the door. Fer took my hand and told me to leave. I stayed anyway.

At five o'clock in the morning, the Holy Night was coming to an end. The tape is a bit damaged and some episodes are irretrievably lost in oblivion. I only remember that Fer was holding my hand, repeating "Merry Christmas... You know I love you so much?" and I was saying, "I love you too, really." "No, I love you in a different way... I love you more than a friend. And in all these months, I didn't know how to tell you."

Then he dropped his glass of wine on the sleeve of my white sweatshirt, began to apologize, and minutes later the conversation began again:

-You know that I love you very much...

-Fer, I love you too, but only as a friend.

-Then I think we'll never see each other again.

-Never again?

-Yes, never again. Every time I see you, I bleed inside.

"I bleed inside." - that son of a bitch saw through me once again. I hated him so much.

A stupid salsa song started to play.

-Well, last dance?- I reached my hand for his.

-Last dance. - he agreed and we started dancing.

The music suddenly hung with its head down, tied to the last note. All the lights went out. The bartender began to chase us feverishly. The code word for the Apocalypse came from somewhere: "Police." Everybody headed for the exit like a group of rats in a hole threatened by a flood. As for me, the world was frightfully frozen. I did not see or hear anything. I just stood there scalded by invisible nettles. Then I felt my knees slowly bend, my body just slid down by itself, and I found myself, by touch, on the couch where I had almost cried.

A rusty voice cracked in the darkness:

-Magnifique! I wish I could dance salsa like that!

Miraculously, I found my jacket, put it on quickly, and replied:

-You can. You just have to be really sad.

People think that salsa music is cheerful to create a happy mood. In fact, it is cheerful to mask the grief. Real salsa dancers bleed on the inside. And the more they bleed, the happier they look.

The man in the darkness laughed. The hollow sound echoed and crashed on the ground like a broken glass.

-Aren't you going to run?- I asked him.

-No, I'll stay. -he replied.

-You're crazy.

-The important thing is that we won.

After the police interrogation, everyone went home. Blanca was going home with Brad's cousin. Somewhere between the birth pains of the Virgin and the sixth hour of Christ's existence, they had gotten engaged, and now they were announcing to everyone they are getting married. Josephine was returning home with William, the Russian with a new archetypal version, this time from the dawn of the turbo-folk, Stefano with a bunch of credit cards, and I… I with Brad. Fer had turned into a chameleon and had crawled unnoticed through the darkness, just before the police got a glimpse of him.

Illegal bars continued to exist, just like cockroaches - the more they were getting smashed, poisoned, suffocated, the more they multiplied. Except that the hiding places were getting wetter, darker, and happier. It seems that all those beast lairs, forgotten even by God, were the perfect place for their full development. For theirs and for ours, of course, their favorite guardian angels.

However, some angels, rumor has it, had broken their wings. Deliberately or not - no one can tell. Probably a bit of both. But before they knew it, new ones had sprouted. They were never like the previous ones, nor did they fly better. They just hurt as they grew and then became beautiful.

I left Sofia and flew to Mexico. My hands got callused from carrying backpacks. I started bleeding only on the outside. I was finally crossing, crossing the globe strenuously and filthily, as I had always wanted. But I never set foot in our bar again. I never won a game of pool again. December 24, 2020 never came again. And of course, never ever again, under no circumstances, did I dare to dance salsa.

The snow, I was told, never fell?

"K" like Becherovka

The first time I met Karin was in 2016. Oh, this crazy 2016!

I wanted to have more of it, to have it last a lifetime.

She met me at the airport. I had just escaped from London. The right word --escaped. My London affair only lasted for 3 months. My little soul couldn't stand this matrix any longer than that. She wanted alcohol, entertainment, and more, if only she knew what. And what could be a better place for a lost soul than Prague?

We met through *couchsurfing*. Yes, that same website where you ask strangers to sleep on their couches. And they accept, if they are crazy enough to do so.

Karin was also a lost soul. She was about to drop out of her bachelor's degree in photography, and I had just dropped out of mine in film directing. Everything promised a wonderful friendship.

Karin got me a drink for a warm welcome. But she really got me drunk. I only remember that she was pouring ungodly amounts of Becherovka into my glass, in some shady thing that resembled a bar, around some crazy people. One of them was a friend of hers with a baby face and blond hair, with whom we repeated that we love each other, and the others I do not remember too well. On leaving the bar, I tried for a long time to put on my jacket, not realizing that it was flipped upside down. Then Karin took me by the arm and dragged me to the subway. On changing lines, I vomited in a trash can. Then we magically found ourselves at her place and I collapsed onto the bed.

The next morning, with a pleasant headache, I hung out at her school because I had to go out with her at eight o'clock in the morning. And with that same headache, we spent the rest of our time planning our miserable lives.

Karin was thinking of returning to Bratislava, where she was actually from, and I didn't know, but I was foretasting a flight to Portugal. One more country where I was intending to ruin my life.

Karin and I never stayed friends. Life scattered us in different directions. She did return to Bratislava and she seemed to have started studying again. Contrary to all my expectations, I betrayed my bohemian spirit and returned to Bulgaria a few months later. (As if I could lead a settled life.)

But again I was madly grieving for the road. I fell into depression, I started, this time, to drink for real. That's when my life of nasty attics, deadly doses of instant coffee and obsessive suicidal thoughts began- nothing to do with settling down. But that's another story. I was making plans of leaving everything behind again, of hitting the endless road again, of finding myself, this time in Beijing, Laos, Los Angeles, on the floor of small cozy places of small crazy people with bottomless dreams in even more cramped quarters, with even more uncomfortable mattresses. Of getting up early, rushing through even more bottomless cities and meeting Karin, Elishka, Jordan in even more bottomless bodies. Of dreams being fragmented again, innocent, torn apart, scattered on the floor like sugar, and sweet, sweet like the air around me. And there will be no more truth, there will be only lies, lies, lies, and I will write, I will write about the despair of the people in different parts of the globe. And just when it becomes ubiquitous, just when I create a network of disappointments, it will break and everyone will get one. Then the world will be happy. And it may not be Prague, but I'll toss Becherovka back in some bottomless trash can at some even more bottomless subway station wearing a crooked jacket upside down. And as ugly as that may seem, everyone will remember, even though they've never been with me, about fucking 2016. And they will die from my own *Saudade*.

By the way, I am currently in Bratislava. But Karin is gone. She would be in Thailand until the end of September. Ten more days and I could see her. But life doesn't wait, Karin. And I don't have all the time in the world anymore. But I still wanted to see you. And in your honor, I bought some Becherovka. Of course, it will not be the same. Because I am neither with you nor in Prague. But mostly because I'm not with you. Now I remember that you took some photos of me just before we got drunk. On some cobbled street, under some yellow December lanterns. You were going to send them, but you never did. I am not mad at you. Don't bother. Is it worth ruining the past? Those would be my only "before and after" photos. Before and after the change.

Because back then something changed in me. It wasn't the alcohol, no, no. Nor those streets. Not even my conversation with you. Or maybe it was all together. Maybe then something was born. Something was born and died at the same time. Some long version of Me had long been waiting for some long version of You to appear and create me as I am at the moment. And that's exactly what I am grieving and drinking for today. Erasing, depersonalizing all photographs from the past. Except the ones that you keep.

Tea without Manushka's Hair

What happens when you are oversaturated, when you have tried all earthly and unearthly pleasures hundreds of times and nothing stirs you up anymore, no girl excites you and no love, when every story, though incredible, seems familiar to you, when your heart doesn't start beating harder even upon meeting an interesting person, what do you do then? Among all this hell of abundance that you have created, you have nothing left but to continue burying yourself. There is no way, and a return the simple life is impossible. Such was the case with Pepe Luis Contreras .

Pepe had been living in Prague for the past seven years, but was initially from Venezuela. There he was married to Paula, a dark-haired Ecuadorian, but one day he found out she was cheating on him and called her a "whore." One morning, sitting behind the desk of his law office, he found a claim against himself. In Venezuela, the laws against domestic violence were very strict and even insulting a woman made you eligible for punishment. At least Pepe got away with it smoothly. All he had to do was go under full-time surveillance and visit a psychiatrist with a group of rapists and men who attempted to kill their wives. He had to repeat the phrase: "Women should not be harassed." fifty times a day and to talk about his relationship with his mother. When it was finally over, he packed his bags and left for Europe. He first lived in Amsterdam, where he fell in love with a Dutch woman. He did not know a word in Dutch, but one day, after all her outbursts in her native language, he finally understood what she was saying. However, he remained silent and diligently prepared his revenge. So during the next battle he cursed her in pure Dutch. She dropped her jaw. From that moment onwards they despised each other so much that they had no choice but to jump into bed and have wild sex. At least that's what Pepe liked to say.

Eventually he got tired of the Dutchwoman, got tired of wild sex and the Venezuelan macho hit the road again. He toured London, Paris, Berlin and finally found himself in Prague. When he realized that the beer and striptease clubs were the cheapest in Europe, he decided to stay there forever. True, he would never be able to find a job as a lawyer. Here, on our continent, he would always be an alien. But still, unforgettable days awaited him. He became a bartender in a nightclub.

Every night turned into a crazy party, every morning into a prelude to the next. Parties from Friday night to the next week. Little by little he got all the diamonds of the night life - discos, bars, casinos… A lot of women, a lot of alcohol and a little bit of drugs.

In the end, he calmed down a little. He turned 30, and that's when every man more or less calms down, at least that's what they say. He didn't go out every night anymore, and on Fridays he didn't even overdo it with alcohol. But he continued to love women. It was easy for him to get their attention – his exotic South American tan, his come-hither smile… He had two and sometimes three dates a day, but he always followed his golden rule - not to deceive them that their relationship was serious, while never letting them find out about the rest.

So when he received Manushka's address –Zelenki Hayski №8 in Zhizhkov Neighborhood, - Pepe bristled. Another of his women, Camilla, also lived there. But he decided to take the risk. Camilla worked an afternoon shift and the date with Manushka was at 5 pm on a weekday. There wasn't even a tiny chance he would cross paths with Camilla's that day.

He rang the doorbell. Manushka ran down the stairs. When she opened the door for him, her freckles shone brighter than usual. The effect of the sun is sometimes strange – it turns some girls into moons. They entered the apartment. It was their first date. Manushka handed him a cup of Thai tea and sat in front of him on the floor. He had the feeling she had dipped her hair into the tea because it too, like the cup, smelled of magnolia. Pepe felt as if he was on his way to one of those exotic countries he'd forgotten to visit. The more Manushka laughed, the more her freckles faded until the moon really rose. And he wondered what would happen then, if the moon in front of him would still shine. She remained the same, only with more dimples. Pepe got so enchanted with Manushka that he even forgot to kiss her. When he left, she took his hand for goodbye. It was warm.

After a few days, the Venezuelan woke up with a strange feeling in his stomach. He didn't feel like doing anything, he didn't even want to eat. His whole body hurt terribly and he felt helpless. He went to the doctor.

Human life is so fragile. You go to the doctor for one thing, but it turns out to be another. And here he is now in front of us- Pepe Luis Contreras.

The same Pepe, but in the final stage of cancer.

When he hears the results, Pepe shudders. A single thought passes his mind: "What if this whole life ends without kissing Manushka?"

For the first time he is terrified. He is not terrified by death, he is terrified by life. He cannot bear the fact that he has lived so much, but he has lived without her.

Manushka learns about Camilla. Her big eyes well up and

turn into craters. She is not angry. She does not hate him. But something in the core of the moon is broken. And here they are now, all those freckles without light.

She goes to the hospital to see him. She is wearing a blue dress and her hair is tucked away. She sits next to him and grabs him by the hand. It is very warm.

"I'm not mad at you," she tells him.

Out of all the things he could hear, this seems to be the most cruel. He feels like crying forever. But he is very weak and can't even make a sound.

Manushka hands him a box of magnolia tea and runs to the door. She feels like crying forever.

On the last day of his life, Pepe drinks tea and thinks: "Even if you just remember the love that didn't come true, even that is worth it."

The Afternoon of Hank or Heinrich

His name is Hank or Heinrich, I'm not sure. When we meet, I don't try to remember his name. This is one of those acquaintances you make out of courtesy. He walks past me with his fishing rod and greets me. I am sitting on the ground in front of this small pond in the woods near Berlin. The weather is calm. The place, too. I come here from time to time to read. Today I'm doing the same. But somehow, I don't feel like reading. No matter how hard I try, my thoughts always fly away somewhere else.

I start talking to Hank or Heinrich.

-What's your name? -I ask him.

-Hank.

or

-Heinrich.

He sinks his fishing rod with a swing. Even though he's focused, he doesn't seem to mind talking.

He sits on his little chair. He wears a hat on his head, one of those buckets with silly ties hanging around his neck. His face is slightly wrinkled, but friendly. He looks about forty, forty-five.

Hank or Heinrich takes a package of peanuts out of his pocket. He grabs a handful, then hands it to me:

-Want some?

-Why not? -I answer.

I don't feel like eating peanuts, but I can't refuse the kind invitation.

There are two types of people in this world - those who eat peanuts in front of you without even offering you one, and those who offer them to you as soon as they open them. Hank or Heinrich is one of the latter.

We talk about insignificant things. He asks me if I study or work. Practically neither, I answer. I am a writer. When he hears the word 'writer', Hank or Heinrich rolls his eyes. I wonder why that is, but then I understand. The truth is they've watered. This doesn't make an impression on me, and anyway, it is not polite to ask him why. Such questions are not to be asked to people who share their package of peanuts with you.

-And you, what do you do?

-I...- Hank or Heinrich startles, as if he has completely forgotten that he is not alone. Then he smiles friendlily at me and adds:

-I'm a supermarket manager.

I don't ask him which supermarket, because at that moment it doesn't matter to me. But now that I think about it, it bothers me a little that I didn't.

-Your house must be full of food.

I make this inappropriate joke just to continue the conversation, because I see that Hank or Heinrich is starting to slip away again.

-Oh, yes.- he replies very seriously. Then, realizing I was joking, he adds:

-Piles of food.

And he makes a funny gesture with his free hand. Then we laugh.

-Someday I'll invite you to visit.-Hank or Heinrich interjects.-My wife makes great apple pie, and if you don't like apple pie, cherry…"

-Who doesn't like apple pie! -I interrupt him.

He laughs again. Then he adds:

-My children, for example. The little one, Cornelia, she's ten, says she's sick of apple pie.

-Surely she's just saying that. At that age children seek attention.

-I thought so, too. But one day she just spat a piece of apple pie out on the table. Since then I don't know…

Then a bird flies past us. I don't think it's important, but

Hank or Heinrich looks at the bird for unusually long time.

Then, when the bird disappears from sight, I realize that Hank or Heinrich is not looking at the bird, but at something else.

Finally, his gaze returns to the fishing rod in the lake. He puts his hand in his pocket and asks:

-Do you smoke?

I answer:

-No.

-Better. I didn't smoke at your age either. But then you know, work, stress…

-I understand.

-Damn it, where's my lighter?

He finds his lighter and lights a cigarette.

-You understand…-he laughs.-Child, you don't understand anything. And you better never understand, if you ask me. One morning you wake up and everything is the same. Your wife sleeps next to you, the children are in the other room getting ready for school. You go to the bathroom to wash yourself. And while brushing your teeth you suddenly realize that you have used the same toothpaste for years. When the tube is empty, you go to the store and buy a new one. Then it's gone and then again… Your teeth start turning yellow and the toothpaste remains white. And this stupid realization makes your hair stand on end, do you understand me? Not that there

is anything scary about using the same toothpaste, but something in you is terrified.

Then you go to the kitchen and drink coffee. Your coffee
is as bitter as always, but now you suddenly start putting a lot
of sugar in it. Your wife says: "Sunshine, since when do you
drink your coffee with sugar?" You don't feel like explaining,
you can't explain. You just want to pour in all the sugar, you
don't want to leave a single crystal. For the first time, you enjoy
burnt toast. And that jam that you were going to throw away
because it's past the expiration date, you spread it on the burnt
bread. Then you take the children to school, you leave them at
school, they say "Bye, Dad." and it makes you happy, but only
for a while, because they get out of sight and stop thinking
about you. You know that this "Bye, dad" doesn't mean anything to them. Then you go to work, some mistress is waiting
for you in your office, forgive me for talking about such things
in front of you, child, you tell her, "I can't now." "When?" "At
eight." You work all day, eight is approaching, you call your
wife to tell her you're going to be late, you go to the mirror to
shave, you go out, you start the car, you go to your mistress's
house, she's already waiting for you in front, and you see how
she's decked out, wearing a tight black dress, heels, her hair is
done. You see all this and you like it, but suddenly something
in you clicks, you don't know what it is, or why, but suddenly
you just pass her by in your car as quickly as possible, so she

won't notice that it's you, or maybe she already has, and that terrifies you, but then, wait, some part of you likes it and with some forgotten adrenaline you fly through the small streets, just the way you were in a hurry to see her before, now you are in a hurry to run away from her, and then you go to the store, buy toothpaste, a new brand, come home grinning, your wife asks you, "So you still managed to finish on time, sunshine?" "That's right." "Then you can have dinner with us." The children are already at the table, there is a duck with mushrooms, and for dessert that apple pie I told you about. You have dinner, you go brush your teeth, this time with the new toothpaste, and go to bed, then your wife calls you out from the bathroom: "Wasn't there any of our regular toothpaste, Sunshine?" God, you want to explain everything. You want to explain to her that there was, but something in you is dying, damn it, you just want to run away from here. You just want to run as long as your breath can hold, and then just drop dead, gutted. It will be better than this life. But you can't, because you have children, obligations and then all you have left to do is buy a new toothpaste. You want to explain all this to her, but you can't. And then you start to feel like the loneliest creature on earth. You scrunch up in the corner of the bed and try to scream as much as your voice can hold. You try to do this, but instead only one thing comes out of your mouth: "No, there wasn't any of our regular toothpaste."

Hank or Heinrich says all this to his fishing rod, not to me, because it clearly seems that he has already forgotten that he has company.

-Everything will be fine.-I mutter.

-Of course.-he answers, too embarrassed that he's said all this aloud.

I don't want to bother him anymore, so I tell him I'm going to finish my book.

He replies:

-Enjoy your book!

And he smiles kindly at me . I do the same.

Then I sit in the grass and start reading. But I am not really doing that because I can't stop thinking about Hank or Heinrich. After a while he starts tugging on his fishing rod. Apparently, at last, something got caught.

A medium-sized fish flops into the hands of Hank or Heinrich. He throws it into the bucket and begins to watch its helpless body toss in all directions. His eyes water. He reaches into the bucket, catches the fish and throws it back into the lake.

But there is something strange about the movement of Hank or Heinrich as he throws the fish back into the lake. As he does so, he jumps there himself.

I get up and run to the shore.

The fish is moving vigorously into the water. The body of Hank or Heinrich is not.

The Sock in Karl Kerstensen's Shoe

The alarm rang, as every morning, at eight o'clock. The six-month day had just begun, so it was not difficult for Karl Kerstensen to wake up. In fact, "wake up" was an overstatement. He had barely managed to take a nap. His eyes still found it hard to adapt to all this light. So it would be for at least another week, as it happened every year.

And though he did whatever it took to isolate himself from the constant day — he had bought black curtains, he drew them all the way, he turned all the lights off, he even glued plastic stars to the ceiling, those stars for children that glow in the dark. But with that blind yet all-seeing eye of animal intuition remaining in us as testament from our ancestors, Karl Kerstensen was aware that it was still unbearably bright outside.

He rubbed his eyes, grabbed his phone from the night-stand, and turned off the alarm. Then he set a new one, but not the same one. He had recently started using a meditation app that worked very effectively. A calm, metallic woman's voice was counting down the seconds, needed to inhale and exhale, and then repeated the action for twenty-five minutes.

Twenty-five minutes. According to the application, that was how long it took for the brain to fully reset.

One last breath was counted and it was time for Karl Kerstensen to get out of bed. He felt his brain completely recovered.

He got dressed and went to the kitchen to make breakfast. As on every morning, he would prepare himself an omelet with cheese. Except that he was out of cheese.

Karl Kerstensen frowned. He knew he had to buy some cheese yesterday, but he still thought there was a little more left, enough for an omelet. He had to make sunny-side-up eggs instead. It wasn't the end of the world. But Karl Kerstensen really loved his cheese omelet for breakfast.

Then it was time to leave for work. He had to hurry, because he had wasted an unusual amount of time preparing the eggs. In general, he was punctual, but now, probably because of the six-month day, it was difficult for him to concentrate.

When he put his left foot in his leather shoe, he felt a sock rubbing his toes. He didn't have time to deal with the damn sock, so he grabbed his briefcase and walked to his car.

He left the briefcase in the front seat next to him. A tag with the name "Karl Kerstensen" hung from its handle, and under it were written his office phone and his personal email. The same information, only in the form of a sticker, was on his laptop, wallet and his subscription card for the Oslo golf course.

Karl Kerstensen stayed in the office all day long. It was busy, but normal. Only one thing bothered Karl Kerstensen all the time. The sock in his shoe irritated him.

Naturally, he could not take off his shoe just like that. Both his colleagues and his clients would be left with a bad impression. He thought of going to the toilet to shake out his shoe, but he never found time to do it during work.

At the end of his shift, Karl Kerstensen could no longer stand it. Although he tried not to pay attention to his sock, suddenly all his attention was focused on it.

He was just like a little kid. "Come on, Karl Kerstensen, tighten up," he repeated to himself. He tried to meditate. Ten seconds of inhaling and ten exhaling. Twenty-five minutes… Shortly before two minutes had passed, his face flushed and small drops of sweat dripped down his forehead.

He had to keep his composure. Colleagues from the neighboring computers were already looking at him out of the corners of their eyes. He knew that they were working only ostensibly, but in fact they were watching to see if others were doing their job. Any moment now they would probably tell the manager that Karl's face was flushing and small drops of sweat were dripping down his forehead. And he wanted to become an assistant manager, so he shouldn't engage in such frivolities, especially because of some sock stuck in his shoe.

His shift was over. That was nice, but he had to stay fifteen minutes longer because he hadn't finished his assignment on time. That ruined the rest of the evening because Karl Kerstensen didn't get a moment after work to shake the sock out of his shoe.

He had a date with a woman from a dating app. She would be waiting for him at the restaurant, but even under those circumstances he was running late, so he immediately got in his car and drove off.

It was the first time Karl Kerstensen had had a date from a dating app. That wasn't his style at all. But his office friends had advised him to give it a try. One of them, Johan, was even married to a girl he met on the same app. More as a joke than seriously, Karl Kerstensen made himself a profile.

We must admit that Karl Kerstensen's imagination, though poor, quickly became excited by the prospect of choosing a woman by photo and description. That was just as convenient as doing online shopping from a furniture store. Everything was detailed and systematic. There was no need to go out before being sure what it is you want.

He had looked at a lot of profiles and sent messages to a couple of women. One of them, an artificial platinum blonde, thirty-four years old, had answered him. She looked good, and Karl Kerstensen was nervous. He would have preferred for one of the less attractive women to answer him, because then the danger of having competitors would be less.

Not that there was anything wrong with Karl Kerstensen. He was a little younger than Nora-- that was the blonde's name. Two and a half years younger, to be exact. His hair was starting to fall, but he was still in a good shape. His abdomen was slightly loose, but within acceptable limits. Medium tall, blue eyes, teeth-yellowish from the coffee he drank all day long, but a decent smile. Expensive leather shoes. Karl Kerstensen couldn't live without his leather shoes.

The blonde was waiting for him at the table.

-Nora.-she said.

-Karl Kerstensen.

They shook hands.

He called her "Nora", but in his mind he was still suspicious. You can never be sure of the true identity of people on those dating apps.

Karl Kerstensen ordered a steak with potato garnish, and Nora ordered an orange shake and pasta with cheese. The conversation went well. There were almost no awkward moments when neither of them knew what to say.

Somewhere in the middle of dinner, between the penultimate potato and Nora's smile, Karl Kerstensen began to get an erection. The candles on the table were illuminating the cheap tablecloth and the enticing décolletage of the lady, and the conversation was continuing in a good direction. All the normal talk about work, which was boring, but could not be exhausted.

Only one thing bothered Karl Kerstensen. The sock stuck in the leather shoe of his left foot.

-Excuse me for a moment.-said Karl Kerstensen.

He headed to the bathroom. He could finally take out the trapped sock.

At first, he thought of doing it in the common space, where the urinals were. But then he decided not to. He was a gentleman, and it was not respectful in front of the other gentlemen to take off, or shake out, his shoes. So he went to the booth.

He closed the door and locked it just in case. Not that he had anything to hide, but it would still be quite embarrassing if any of the other gentlemen saw him there, all angry, sitting on the toilet bowl shaking out his shoe.

The sock fell. It smelled disgusting. It smelled of something much more unpleasant than a long-used sock. Karl Kerstensen jumped up off the toilet bowl. Not that there was anything so scary to jump up for, but Karl Kerstensen was surprised. That was actually not a sock. It was a dead mouse.

Karl Kerstensen pinched his nose with one hand and grabbed the mouse by the tail with the other. He tossed it into the toilet and flushed it.

He watched in horror and satisfaction as its little body spun, covered in foam, and finally disappeared from his sight forever.

He washed his hands for a long time and then returned to Nora. His steak was almost finished. A few more bites and they were ready to go.

He invited her to his house. She agreed. They got in his car. On the way home, Karl Kerstensen was nervous. What if mice had infested his house? It would be very embarrassing if some mouse jumped out, especially in Nora's presence.

They went to his bedroom. Karl Kerstensen looked around.

-What's wrong?- Nora asked.

Karl Kerstensen looked nervous to her.

-Is everything all right?-she repeated.

Karl Kerstensen did not answer. They sat on the bed and started kissing.

Nora undressed Karl Kerstensen and Karl Kerstensen undressed Nora. Nora was beautiful. She had soft skin and her hair, though dyed, gave her some kind of natural innocence.

Nora saw that Karl Kerstensen was still nervous, so she sat on top. But instead of getting more aroused, Karl Kerstensen lost his entire erection.

Here's something about Karl Kerstensen that neither Nora nor even his friends knew. Karl Kerstensen didn't like having sex.

It was unusual for him when his friends talked about sex with excitement. Karl Kerstensen was neither a virgin nor a homosexual. It was just that sexual intimacy did not bring him pleasure.

People are so used to identifying everything with sex and sexuality that if they are absent from someone's life, they become automatically separated from regular humanity. But Karl Kerstensen had never wanted to stand out as an individual. If he invited Nora home, it was because it was accepted to do so. But deep down he had hoped Nora would refuse.

Of course, that didn't make Karl Kerstensen less of a human. He, like most people, wanted to have a relationship. He wanted to have a woman by his side, no matter what she looked like, as long as she supported and understood him. He wanted normal human things. Kiss on the shoulder in the morning, someone to make him an omelet with cheese, and in the evening, when going to bed, to have someone to cuddle with while trying to fall asleep.

But all the women wanted something more from him that he just couldn't give them.

Nora was lying on the other side of the bed crying.

-It's not your fault.-said Karl Kerstensen.

-I'm getting old.

-Nothing like that.

-My breasts are starting to sag and I already have cellulite.

- I think you are very beautiful.

- There's no point in lying to me.

-I really think you're beautiful.

-Then why don't you want me?

Nora's eyes were the same as Karl Kerstensen's and those of most Norwegians. But her eyes looked like they were made of glass that shone in the sun. Karl Kersensen had forgotten to draw the curtains.

Karl Kerstensen didn't answer her question.

Nora went to draw the curtains.

-When I was twelve years old, somebody tried to rape me. I was at a summer camp and he was a teacher there. One day he called me to his room and took off my pants. He said these are normal things that friends do. I told him I didn't like it, but he kept convincing me. He tried to give me a blowjob. He tried to do other things I won't tell you about right now. I was scared. I told him I didn't like it, but he kept going. I was lucky because then someone knocked on the door. He pulled my pants back up and told me to promise him I would not tell anyone. A woman came into the room and asked us what we were doing. She saw the tears in my eyes. He said that I had scraped my knee and I had come to ask him to put a bandage on it. He turned to me and asked: "Right?". I said: "Yes." Then I went out, but I was no longer crying. Since then I haven't liked to have sex,–Karl said.

Nora was still crying. She hugged Karl. Karl hugged Nora. And just like that, accidentally, they fell asleep together.

About the Author

But this frantic need to break myself down, to dismember myself into pieces, is nothing more than a longing for life. Longing is too thin of a word and can hardly express my true feeling for this obsession. I would rather call it lust, animal lust to possess life.

I want to tear every layer of myself, because man, like everything in nature, is made of thousands of layers. And to peel off what we at first sight see as apparent wholeness, that which we all consider to be our essence. There are thousands of other people somewhere in me, and each of them is begging me, like a little animal, to shelter them in what they call inner world. There is no space for more, I can only remove and destroy to make room for the new inhabitants.

That is why I die so often.

I discover new animals every day. Some of them want to

completely destroy the others. They want to rule in full force, they want to subdue even me, their master.

Others are very weak and gentle. But there is justice in the inner world - it is the exact opposite of the outer one. That's why I don't allow anyone to kill the latter. I just sometimes hide them from the others so they can really survive.

The more I delve into myself, the more I discover that I will never find me. I just give room for new creatures, like the gardener shovels the soil to plant new seeds.

My garden is dense and lush. Sometimes I go with the mower, cut everything off and start all over. But very soon I discover that instead of tearing weeds, I plucked only flowers from eyes, spleens and knees. And unable to put them back into their places, I throw everything together on one big canvas without a name. I would like to say this is me, but this is not me either.

Fomite

Writing a review on social media sites for readers will help the progress of independent publishing. To submit a review, go to the book page on any of the sites and follow the links for reviews. Books from independent presses rely on reader-to-reader communications.

For more information or to order any of our books, visit:
http://www.fomitepress.com/our-books.html

More story collections from Fomite...

MaryEllen Beveridge — After the Hunger
MaryEllen Beveridge — Permeable Boundaries
Jay Boyer — Flight
L. M Brown — Treading the Uneven Road
L. M Brown — Were We Awake
Michael Cocchiarale — Here Is Ware
Michael Cocchiarale — Still Time
Neil Connelly — In the Wake of Our Vows
Catherine Zobal Dent — Unfinished Stories of Girls
Zdravka Evtimova — Carts and Other Stories
John Michael Flynn — Off to the Next Wherever
Derek Furr — Semitones
Derek Furr — Suite for Three Voices
Elizabeth Genovise — Where There Are Two or More
Andrei Guriuanu — Body of Work
Zeke Jarvis — In A Family Way
Arya Jenkins — Blue Songs in an Open Key
Bobby Johnston — The Saint I Ain't
Jan English Leary — Skating on the Vertical
Julia MacDonnell— The Topography of Hidden Stories
Marjorie Maddox — What She Was Saying
William Marquess — Badtime Stories
William Marquess — Because Because Because Because Because

Fomite

William Marquess — Boom-shacka-lacka
William Marquess — Things I Want You to Do
Gary Miller — Museum of the Americas
Jennifer Anne Moses — Visiting Hours
Charles Opara — How Hamisu Survived Bad Kidneys
and a Bad Son-in-Law
Martin Ott — Interrogations
George Ovitt — The Showcase
Christopher Peterson — Amoebic Simulacra
Christopher Peterson — Scratch the Itchy Teeth
Charles Phillips — Dead South
Jack Pulaski — Love's Labours
Charles Rafferty — Saturday Night at Magellan's
Joseph Rathgeber — Bad Days on the Batso
Mohsen Rezaei — The Violet Needle
Ron Savage — What We Do For Love
Vince Sgambati — Undertow of Memory
Fred Skolnik— Americans and Other Stories
Lynn Sloan — This Far Is Not Far Enough
L.E. Smith — Views Cost Extra
Caitlin Hamilton Summie — To Lay To Rest Our Ghosts
Susan Thomas — Among Angelic Orders
Tom Walker — Signed Confessions
Silas Dent Zobal — The Inconvenience of the Wings